"Please don't love me, Erin," Nick said

His voice sharpened. "I can't take the responsibility."

"There's no responsibility," Erin cried. "I love you. You don't have to do anything but accept it."

Nick sighed deeply, grasping her shoulders firmly.

"I can't let you love me," he said, "when I have nothing to give you. I can't tell you I love you, and even if I could, you couldn't believe it. Tomorrow, the day after, whenever—if ever—my memory returns, it might suddenly become a lie. I don't know who I am or what I've done—so how can you trust me, let alone love me?"

"But I do." Erin knew she'd trusted him from the moment he'd stopped their lovemaking—for her sake—that first night. "And I love the person you are. Nothing else matters!"

KATE WALKER chose the Brontë sisters, the development of their writing from childhood to maturity, as the topic for her master's thesis. It is little wonder, then, that she should go on to write romance fiction. She lives in the United Kingdom with her husband and son, and when she isn't writing, she tries to keep up with her hobbies of embroidery, knitting, antiques and, of course, reading.

Game of Hazard

Kate Walker

Harlequin Books

TORONTO • NEW YORK • LONDON
AMSTERDAM • PARIS • SYDNEY • HAMBURG
STOCKHOLM • ATHENS • TOKYO • MILAN

Original hardcover edition published in 1986
by Mills & Boon Limited

ISBN 0-373-02783-4

Harlequin Romance first edition August 1986

For Steve

CHAPTER ONE

THE ginger cat was sitting on the doorstep of the cottage, huddled tightly into one corner, as far away from the whirling snow as possible. Erin saw the bright splash of colour his fur made against the white as she rounded the corner into the narrow, rutted lane that led to her home. There was nothing unusual in his being there, Rufus often waited for her return from Forlcy village in just this position; but what stopped her dead in her tracks and sent a shiver through her that had nothing to do with the bitterly cold wind blowing across the moors was the firm conviction that when she had left the house almost two hours before, the cat had been inside, curled up safe and warm on the rug before the fire.

Erin hesitated, her clear hazel eyes troubled as she relived the last few minutes before she had left the cottage. She had dressed as warmly as possible, well aware of the snowfall threatening in the heavy, dull grey sky, tucking her jeans down inside her boots, adding a navy duffle coat and a bright red knitted hat that concealed every wayward curl of her light brown hair. Then she had collected her shopping list and several bags, the bags that now lay at her feet, filled to overflowing with provisions, checked that the fire was safe and banked up with enough coal to last while she was out and—yes!—the scene came vividly to her mind—she had paused to stroke Rufus before starting out reluctantly on the long trek to the village.

Erin shifted uneasily where she stood, stamping her feet against the cold. She was tired, her arms ached from carrying the bags, and the icy wind had chilled her through to the bone. She wanted desperately to be inside, thinking longingly of a hot cup of coffee and the comforting glow of the coal fire. But if Rufus was outside when she had left him safely in the house then, unless the cat had suddenly acquired the knack of opening the stiff and ill-fitting front door—and closing it behind him—someone else had to be inside the cottage. Someone had entered her home while she was away shopping in Forley, accidentally letting the cat out in the process.

For the first time Erin was forced to doubt her own decision to choose such an isolated spot in which to live. When she had first seen Moor End Cottage, knowing that it was hers, it had been on a mild and mellow September afternoon and then the small house had seemed a delightful place, quite perfect in fact, offering her the peace and sanctuary she longed for. But now, almost three months later, with the snow rapidly obscuring what little was left of the track that was so exaggeratedly described as Moor End Road, and the gloom of a winter evening closing in around her, she realised with a shudder just how very vulnerable she was out here on her own and recalled her father's shocked horror when he saw her new home.

'You're not living here!' he had exclaimed. 'Erin, darling, it's the back of beyond! There isn't a soul for miles.'

'But that's what I've always loved about it!' Erin protested. 'You can't imagine how peaceful it seems after my flat in Leeds—you'd have to have lived in that place to believe how noisy it was. I'm not a big city girl, Dad; Moor End suits me just fine. I can work here with nothing to disturb me—no phone, no callers, just me.'

And no Geoff, she added silently, not trusting herself to say the words out loud though she knew her father would understand if she did.

'I still don't see why you won't work for me. You

could live at home then and have an office at the mill——'

'And spend quiet evenings at home with you and Elaine?' Erin could not prevent the sharpness creeping into her voice when she spoke of her stepmother. 'No Dad, you know that would never work out; the only thing Elaine and I have in common is you. Moor End is my home now.'

'Very well,' Jack Howarth sighed. 'But you must promise me you'll keep in touch. I'm not at all happy at the thought of you living in some Wuthering Heights of a place like this.'

Her father's words echoed round and round in Erin's head as she stood shivering with indecision and cold, staring at the cottage that had been home to her for just a few short weeks, wondering just what she would find if she was to venture inside. She had been so determined to get away from the comfortable routine, a routine that had suddenly seemed so empty because one important part of it was missing, that she had not considered the possibility of anything like this happening. The cottage itself offered her no clues as to the possibility of there being an intruder within its walls. No lights shone from the small, old-fashioned windows, so that they stared out at the deepening snowdrifts like blank, sightless eyes, and the gathering dusk gave the small house an insubstantial and disturbingly eerie appearance.

With a sigh Erin drew herself up and squared her shoulders. She would freeze if she didn't move soon; it was time she made a decision. She had to go into the cottage and risk whatever she might find there—it was either that or trekking the two miles back to the village. Neither prospect particularly appealed.

A sudden fierce gust of wind and the swirling of the snow across her path so that Moor End almost disappeared from view made up Erin's mind for her.

After all, she told herself firmly, she was probably making a drama out of nothing. Rufus could move like a streak of ginger lightning when he wanted to; he could easily have sneaked past her legs and out into the garden.

It was only when she reached the shelter of the doorway, her key in her hand, that Erin looked closely at the door and froze, her arm still outstretched.

The door was not fully closed. A gap of an inch or more showed between it and the doorpost and as Erin pushed at it lightly with her foot it swung open slowly with a faint protesting creak of the hinges. Erin could not move. She could not take one step into the house that had earlier appeared so welcoming but now seemed to harbour unknown dangers.

'H—hello!' she called quaveringly, her voice rising and falling unnaturally. 'Is there anyone there?'

A silence broken only by the howling of the wind greeted her tentative call. She swallowed nervously, taking several deep breaths to calm herself, but failed to slow the frantic pounding of her heart that seemed to be beating high up in her throat. With an effort she forced herself to consider the dim hallway, screwing up her eyes against the gloom.

Nothing seemed to have been touched or disturbed; even her radio still stood on the hall table. If a thief had broken in then surely that would have gone, Erin thought, relief making her suddenly lightheaded so that she almost laughed aloud at her own fears. The radio-cassette player was brand new, a recent birthday present from her father. It was an expensive model, compact and easily movable—just the sort of thing a thief would pick up at once.

It was all right! There was no one there! The swift release from the tension that had gripped her from the moment she had first seen Rufus on the doorstep left Erin feeling limp and she sagged back against the doorpost to recover her composure. Rufus snaked past her ankles, heading straight for the kitchen door at the end of the hall. As Erin watched he hooked a claw into the heavy wood, pulling determinedly until at last the door swung open and he disappeared triumphantly into the kitchen in search of food.

This time Erin did not restrain the laughter that bubbled up inside her and escaped in a soft chuckle. The cat had just demonstrated exactly how he had got out of the house without her help. The front door stuck badly, it often needed force to close it properly. She must have left it very slightly ajar when she had gone out and with a great deal of patience and determination Rufus had pulled it open and the wind had blown it shut behind him.

Filled with a new energy, she shrugged off the last of her hesitation and strode briskly into the hall, thankfully dropping her bags on to the floor. With the door firmly closed behind her she pulled the two strong bolts across, too, as a belated concession to her earlier fears, vowing silently to herself that never again would she leave the house without checking that the door was firmly locked behind her. She might not be so lucky next time.

'Well, at least that's shut properly now!' she murmured aloud.

The door to the living room stood ajar and Erin glanced in as she passed, a contented smile curving her lips at the sight of the small, cosy room bathed in the warm glow of the fire.

It was good to be home, she thought, tugging off her boots and reaching for her slippers. Let the weather do its worst, she didn't care! The snow could pile up six feet deep outside and she would be perfectly happy. She had anticipated the blizzard that was now raging and had made plans accordingly. There was enough coal and food to see her through even a lengthy siege and she was not afraid of being alone. She had plenty of work to occupy her time and Rufus was all the company she needed.

Erin hummed light-heartedly as she drew the thick velvet curtains across the window, shutting out the bleak prospect of the darkening garden, then flicked a switch, flooding the room with light. At once her bright, cheerful mood vanished, her hand going instinctively to her mouth to still the cry of alarm that rose to her lips as she stared with wide, fearful eyes at the coat that lay on the settee.

It was a navy blue jacket, thickly padded and clearly masculine in design, alien and somehow threatening against the floral chintz cushions. It lay half across one arm of the settee, apparently slung there carelessly or impatiently with complete indifference to the fact that it was soaked right through and the water that had dripped from it was already darkening the cushions against which it lay.

Panic paralysed Erin and it was with a supreme effort that she dragged her eyes away from the jacket and glanced hurriedly around the room, terrified that the owner of the coat might be hiding somewhere, unseen in the half-light. But the room was empty. No dark figure emerged from behind the door or the shadows beside the bookcase and the house was as silent as before. But that silence which Erin had found so welcoming now seemed disturbing, ominous, and filled with an unseen menace. The man who had worn that jacket had to be somewhere; she could have little doubt that he was still here, in her house.

Holding her body tensely, Erin moved to the fireplace, edging uneasily past the settee as if she feared that the navy jacket might come alive, that a hand might emerge from beneath it and grab her as she passed. With hands that were distinctly unsteady she grasped the poker that lay on the hearth and gripped it tightly, drawing new strength from the weight and solidity of the metal beneath her fingers. A small flame of anger lit up inside her, burning away some of the fear. This was her home! No one had the right to walk in, dumping their coat as if the place belonged to them. No one! She was not completely defenceless, not some frail old lady like Great Aunt Bee who had lived at Moor End for over twenty years—and survived. She was young and strong and she was going to find this unwanted intruder and turn him out into the snow—preferably without the coat that had betrayed him!

Moving silently in her slippers, the poker held up before her like a sword, Erin investigated the ground floor of the cottage. This did not take long for Moor End only possessed two other downstairs rooms – the cramped and old-fashioned kitchen and a small back room, officially the dining room. Normally this was her favourite place in the house but now Erin felt none of her usual pleasure in surveying the small, compact workroom she had created for herself. It was as if the house had been contaminated by the presence of the unknown and, as yet, unseen man.

Erin's courage almost deserted her when, after switching on the hall light, she saw what the gloom of the late afternoon had hidden from her before—large, muddy footprints across the wooden floor, crossing to the living room then back through the hall and up the stairs. He had been there all the time, had probably hidden as soon as he heard her arrive. Erin's stomach contracted painfully at the thought of him standing silently in the darkness, listening, waiting. Who was he? A teenage punk perhaps, with wild orange hair? Or an older man, a tramp in his late fifties or sixties?

Well, this is where you get off, Mr Whoever-you-are, she thought grimly, her grip tightening convulsively around the poker. This is my house and you are definitely not welcome!

The floorboards creaked betrayingly as she climbed the stairs but there was no sound from any of the rooms that opened on to the narrow landing. Unwillingly Erin had to admit that the unwelcome intruder was a cool customer; not by the faintest rustle had he given himself away. If he had not been careless and left his coat downstairs she would never even have suspected his presence.

The bathroom door stood wide open and in the light from the landing Erin could see that there was nowhere a man could hide in the small room; that left only the two bedrooms. She debated with herself which one to try first, reluctant to enter either one because that meant turning her back on the door to the other. Then, impatient now to confront her unknown opponent, she kicked open the nearest door and surveyed her own bedroom swiftly, smiling slightly wryly in spite of her nervousness as the action reminded her irresistibly of many detective films she had seen.

But this was no film, and she was no Clint Eastwood or Charles Bronson, she reminded herself, her courage seeping away with every second that passed. Buoyed up by her anger, she hadn't paused to consider what she was actually going to do when she came face to face with the intruder. It was one thing to decide in the heat of the moment to confront him and, hopefully, to drive him out of the house, quite another to know, after a hurried examination of her room that included the huge old wardrobe and a quick glance under the bed, that there was only one room left and he had to be in it.

She couldn't give in now. For one thing it would be impossible to go downstairs knowing exactly where he was but never having seen him. Breathing a heartfelt, if rather despairing prayer that, knowing he was detected, the intruder might have opened a window and, abandoning his jacket, made his escape into the night,

Erin opened the door and peered cautiously into the room, every muscle held taut, ready for defence or flight. The bedroom was silent in the dim light, the whirling snowflakes making strange, shadowy patterns on the carpet, patterns that were repeated, shifting, constantly changing, on the shirt and face of the man who was lying on the bed.

He was fast asleep, sleeping so deeply that he did not stir at the sound of the door opening and made no move as Erin crept soft-footed into the room, never taking her eyes off his still figure for a moment.

Closing the door behind her, Erin leaned back against it, her legs trembling beneath her, her tension giving way to a quivering sensation of doubt mixed with anti-climax. Whatever she had expected it had not been this; not this exhausted, total unconsciousness that had so completely overwhelmed the man on the bed that he was oblivious of her presence even when she moved to switch on the bedside lamp in order to see him more clearly. Stunned and bewildered, she studied the man before her, instinctively keeping a firm grip on the poker in case he should waken. At first, the figure on the bed seemed to blur before her eyes. She had a confused impression of a long, powerful frame, broad shoulders and a slightly unkempt mane of hair, very dark against the white pillow. Then she got a grip on herself and, edging a little nearer, she shook her head to clear the confusion from her mind and looked down at him again.

So much for the punk and the tramp! This man was neither of those. Erin could not guess at his exact age but she thought that, if pressed, she would say thirty, thirty-five, no more. He was no immature youth, that was certain; no one acquired the deep lines that were scored into his face even when relaxed in sleep without experience of the harsher aspects of life. He was a tough-looking character all right, but he did not look like any of her preconceived ideas of a thief or a housebreaker.

Erin smiled ruefully at her own foolishness. What did she expect? That he would be wearing a black mask, a black and white striped jumper and carrying a bag marked 'Swag' like some child's imaginary vision of a burglar?

Grow up! she told herself sharply. Don't let a good-looking face deceive you!

For he was good-looking, there was no denying that. His face was too thin, drawn and gaunt, all sharp angles, his profile sharply defined against the pale pillow-cases, showing clearly the firm line of his jaw, but for all that he was an arrestingly handsome creature with a rugged magnetism that, even in her present distinctly unnerving situation, Erin acknowledged as the sort of appeal most women would find irresistible. She wondered what colour his eyes were under the tightly closed lids.

He was wearing a plain white shirt, very clean, Erin noted automatically, in fact probably brand new, with rather worn denim jeans that were soaked through from ankle to knee as if he had been wading through snowdrifts to reach the house—which he probably had; there had been no sign of a car. There were no shoes on his feet, which was vaguely puzzling until, moving even closer, Erin stumbled over a pair of boots placed neatly side by side at the foot of the bed. Irrationally she found this small fact rather comforting. It was not the act of a vandal to stop and consider the damage his muddy boots would do to the handmade patchwork quilt that covered the bed and her attitude towards this mysterious intruder softened slightly at the thought. A second later she had pulled herself up. Such thinking was dangerous!

The slight sound she had made when she tripped over the boots disturbed the man and he stirred in his sleep, muttering something unintelligible and rolling over on to his back as he did so. The heavy dark hair fell away from his forehead and a shocked gasp escaped Erin as she saw the ugly gash just above his eye. It was perhaps three inches long, a jagged, shallow cut, with a bruise already disfiguring the skin on either side of the wound. It had clearly bled quite a bit at first; there was a trickle of dried blood down the man's left temple and another streak of red across his cheek, but the bleeding had stopped now and there was no stain or mark on the pillow where his head had lain. Still, he was going to find it pretty sore when he finally woke.

That thought brought Erin's attention back to her own situation with a jolt. Just how had he been hurt? Had there been an accident—or a fight? His injury altered things slightly; after a bang on the head like that he could hardly have been thinking too clearly. He might have stumbled into the house in the belief it belonged to someone he knew. So should she be prepared to face some hostile, aggressive man or someone bewildered and confused by the mistake he had made?

'What *am* I going to do with you?'

Without thinking, Erin spoke the words out loud, addressing them to the man on the bed and, as if in response, he stirred again, moving his head restlessly on the pillow.

'No,' he muttered thickly. 'No more—too many—too damn many . . .'

His voice faded away on a sigh so deep, so despondent, that something in it pulled at Erin's heart. What could he be dreaming about? Whatever it was, it was not a pleasant dream seemingly, but a nightmare from which he would be only too glad to wake. Briefly she considered rousing him, then rejected the idea at once. He was still an unknown quantity, an intruder who had entered her home unlawfully, and he was a powerful looking man. It might be the coward's way out but she was not prepared to risk the consequences if he was startled into wakefulness.

Well, he looked as if he would sleep for hours yet. Erin shivered. The room was distinctly chilly, for Moor End had no form of central heating. Acting on an impulse that came from her heart and not her head, she reached for the spare blanket that lay folded across the foot of the bed, opened it out and laid it over the sleeping man. Even in his sleep he sensed its warmth and pulled it closer with a faint sigh. This strangely vulnerable action, like that of a sleeping child, contrasted dramatically with the hard strength of his face and once again Erin felt that touch of sympathy tugging at her heart. But in a blinding moment of realisation she registered just what she had done, the thought bringing a wave of panic that made her head swim. What on earth had possessed her! She stared in horror at the blanket she had so unthinkingly laid over the man on the bed, made a move to snatch it away again, then hesitated, terrified of waking him.

Suddenly she couldn't bear to be in the same room as the intruder a moment longer. Her mind reeled in disbelief at her own foolishness as she fled from the room and almost fell down the stairs in a headlong dash for the door, her heart thudding painfully. She couldn't handle this on her own—she had to get help!

Her hands fumbled with the bolts and the ill-fitting door seemed to resist her attempts to pull it open but at last it yielded and, yanking her coat from its hook, she stumbled out into darkness. The snow was worsening now and Erin was half blinded by the whirling flakes that bombarded her face with stinging coldness. Too late she realised that in her haste she had come out still wearing only her slippers; already her feet were soaked and frozen, but she was not going back! Her hasty flight from the room might have wakened the sleeping man; she had to get away as quickly as possible.

Doggedly Erin put one foot in front of another, ploughing her way through the snowdrifts, trying to distract her thoughts from the aching coldness in her hands and feet by returning to the problem of the mysterious stranger. What accident or action of fate had brought him here like this? How had he been hurt? Had he simply fallen, losing his footing in the treacherous snow, or . . . Erin's head came up sharply— the situation became more complicated the more she thought about it! Perhaps he had been in a car, it would be so easy to crash in the atrocious weather conditions, and she had no guarantees that the man she had found was the only person involved! *He* was safe, if rather bruised and battered, but was anyone else lying hurt somewhere?

Erin felt sick at the thought then gave a cry of alarm as her feet slid from under her and she fell forward into a particularly heavy snowdrift. Gasping harshly she dragged herself upright, brushing the snow from her face with numb fingers. If only she had a phone, then she could have called the police as soon as she discovered that incriminating jacket and handed the whole matter over to them!

Tears burned Erin's eyes as she recalled her father's shocked dismay at the discovery that the cottage did not possess a telephone. He had wanted to pay to have one installed but, in her determination to keep her newly-won independence, Erin had rejected the offer in spite of the fact that a phone would have been useful, sparing her the walk to Forley Post Office when she wanted to contact any of her customers. But in the warmth of early September the journey to the village had seemed no problem at all; now the two miles seemed more like two hundred.

Her breath sobbing in her throat, Erin paused and glanced back the way she had come and groaned aloud at the realisation that she had covered no more than thirty yards—and already she was exhausted. Her jeans were soaked from thigh to ankle and her sodden slippers were like blocks of ice around her feet. Ahead of her she could see nothing; the snow had completely obliterated the track that was Moor End Road and the black night was closing in fast. She floundered forward, panting heavily as she forced her way through the snow, but after only a few steps was forced to halt again. The drifts were getting deeper all the time; at any moment she could find herself up to her waist in them.

The wind buffeted her head until she felt dazed and sick, she could hardly see a yard in front of her and the lights of Moor End were the only landmark she recognised. Every trace of the anger she had felt earlier had drained away, taking with it the welcome courage it had fired.

'Oh, help! Please help me someone!' she cried aloud, knowing even as she did so that there was no one to hear her call.

Exhausted and trembling, Erin faced the truth. She could not go on. She risked freezing to death if she ventured further in these arctic conditions—but her home was no refuge either; there, too, she faced danger. No, she *couldn't* go back! But even as she told herself that, she knew she had no choice. There wasn't a single house on the road to Forley and already she had lost almost all feeling in her legs and feet. At least inside, in the light and warmth, she would have *some* chance. With a choking sound of despair Erin turned back towards the house.

The same eerie silence as before greeted Erin as she stumbled into the kitchen, shivering uncontrollably. Presumably the man upstairs was still asleep, but sooner or later he must wake and when he did . . . Erin clutched the edge of the sink for support. She needed some form of protection—but what?

With sudden determination she opened a drawer and took out a small, sharp knife, sliding it into the pocket of her jeans. If she was really honest with herself she doubted that she would ever have the nerve to use such a weapon, even if she was threatened with violence, but just to know it was there, for use in an emergency, made her feel that little bit stronger.

She had to keep busy—and keep her strength up, Erin told herself firmly. If she sat here waiting, listening for the first sound of movement upstairs, she would go mad! The faint, dull-headed feeling that stopped her thinking clearly was the result of her exhaustion combined with hunger. She had prepared a casserole earlier in the day; all she had to do was put it in the oven—that took care of the food situation. Then she was going into the living room and—Erin's fingers curled in distaste at the thought—she was going to go through that wretched man's pockets and see if she could find some clue to his identity. If she even had a name to give him it would be something.

The silence began to prey on Erin's nerves, every creak of the floorboards making her start in panic, so that she switched on the radio simply to distract herself. The sound of the music helped a little, though if anyone had asked her afterwards what records had been played she would not have been able to tell them.

Against the blackness of the night her own reflection stared back at her from the window above the sink. It showed a slender, rather frail figure in a white sweater splashed with vivid scarlet flowers, her own work and one of her favourite designs, but that thought gave her no pleasure as she gazed at her pale, tense face framed with a halo of soft brown curls.

The girl she saw had wide, apprehensive-looking eyes fringed with naturally thick, dark lashes above a generous, normally smiling mouth. But she was not smiling now; her lips looked stiff and wooden with the effort of holding back the fear she was feeling. She looked very young and defenceless, the independent, confident young woman of twenty-two stripped away, leaving a lost and frightened child in her place.

'Oh Dad,' she whispered. 'Why didn't I listen to you?'

If only she had given in on the issue of the telephone as her father had wanted her to! The police could have been here by now—here and gone again—taking the man upstairs with them, leaving her home safe and secure as before. Or would she ever feel quite so confident about being alone after this? If this man could walk in so easily then . . . Erin shuddered convulsively, her head bent and her eyes swimming with weak, terrified tears. Behind her, the radio chattered on.

'It's seven o'clock and here is the news. Fears are growing for the safety of the three British host——'

The newsreader's voice snapped off abruptly, cut off in mid-sentence, and Erin's head jerked up. In the sudden silence she felt a cold, shivering sensation at the top of her spine as if the tiny hairs on the back of her neck had lifted in the instinctive reaction of a wary cat. She did not have to turn her head to know who was behind her; she could sense his presence with every nerve in her body. He must have come into the room with the soft, sure-footed tread of a hunting tiger for she hadn't heard a sound until the radio had been so abruptly switched off.

Moving very slowly, Erin slid her hand into her pocket, closing her fingers around the handle of the knife before she swung round to face him.

CHAPTER TWO

HE was standing just inside the doorway, very big and dark, appearing much more imposing now that he was on his feet. The dim light of the bedside lamp had disguised the fact that his skin was darkly tanned, something that seemed very much at odds with the howling blizzard outside. His hands were thrust deep into the pockets of his jeans and his very stance, the tautness of every muscle, and a watchful, guarded expression in his eyes revealed a wariness like that of a wild animal scenting a trap.

The man's eyes narrowed swiftly as Erin turned to face him. Earlier she had wondered what colour they might be; now she saw that they were very blue, a clear, cold blue without any hint of warmth in it. They swept over her in a swift, coolly appraising glance that made Erin feel quite irrationally that he had seen right through to her innermost being, probed her most secret thoughts, and then dismissed her as totally unimportant. She felt the anger begin to burn inside her at his behaviour and welcomed it gladly. If she could stay angry she had more chance of being able to cope with this nightmarish situation, though seeing him there, darkly intimidating in the confined space of the tiny kitchen, she seriously doubted that she would have any chance at all if he was the criminal she had suspected at first. At long last the man spoke.

'Do you mind telling me where the hell I am?' he said quietly enough but with a hard, aggressive note in his voice. 'And who, dear lady, are you?'

Erin's chin came up determinedly and she met those narrowed blue eyes without flinching.

23

'I think that's my question!' she said sharply. 'After all, I live here. You're the one who walked in uninvited!'

One dark eyebrow lifted slightly at her tone, drawing Erin's attention to the raw-looking wound on the man's forehead. Seeing the direction of her gaze, he raised one hand almost defensively to the cut, wincing slightly as he touched it, and Erin caught the flash of a heavy gold signet ring on the third finger of his right hand. He had long, fine-boned, but powerful-looking hands, she noted irrelevantly, beautifully shaped hands. With a distinct effort she dragged her attention back to reality. He still had not answered her question.

'Well?' she persisted, eyeing him warily. 'You do have a name I suppose?'

'Oh yes,' came the smoothly spoken response. 'If it's so important to you to know.'

'Then what is it?'

'Nick,' he supplied succinctly.

'Nick what?' Erin snapped, but he shrugged his shoulders indifferently.

'Just Nick—or so my watch tells me.'

'Your watch?' Erin was totally confused. 'What has your watch got to do with this?'

'Everything,' the man called Nick replied cryptically, infuriating Erin further.

'Now look——' she began, but Nick broke in on her.

'No, you look,' he said, pulling back his shirt cuff to reveal an elegant and clearly expensive gold wristwatch which he unfastened and held out to Erin.

'Take it!' he commanded when she hesitated, not at all sure this was not a trap, a trick to get her to move nearer so that he could grab her. Nick thrust the watch towards her again and automatically she took it, snatching at it swiftly, then held it awkwardly, unsure of what to do next.

'On the back, turn it over,' Nick instructed curtly and

in a daze Erin did as she was told. She saw an engraved inscription. 'To Nick on his twenty-first', and a date some twelve years earlier, and her head came up swiftly, her eyes flashing fire.

'Is this your idea of a joke?' she demanded furiously, dropping the watch back into his palm with an abrupt, angry movement. 'I asked you a question, I want a proper answer. Just who are you and what——?'

But Nick had turned away, his blue eyes scanning the kitchen, looking for something.

'Where did I leave my coat?' he broke in on her.

'In the living room,' Erin responded automatically. 'Now just a minute!' she added protestingly as he moved towards the door, 'I think you owe me some sort of an explanation!'

Nick swung round again, turning the full force of those clear, cold eyes on her, and Erin faltered, her throat feeling dry and constricted so that she had difficulty speaking again.

'I mean——' she began but could get no further.

'What do you want to know?' Nick asked evenly.

'What do you think I want to know?' Erin spluttered, her hands curling frustratedly at her sides. The man's immovable calm was maddening! She had to struggle to resist the impulse to take hold of him and shake him until he told her just what he was doing in her home. 'Just how did you get in here for a start?'

The firm, hard mouth curled very slightly at the corners into a faint, mocking echo of a smile.

'You left the door unlocked,' he told her coolly. 'Very careless of you—I just walked in.'

'You just walked in!' Erin exploded, feeling as if the room was spinning round her. This crazy conversation did not make sense. *He* was the one who she had thought might be confused and apologetic, but an apology seemed the furthest thing from this man's mind and Erin herself was the one who was confused.

'Is that all you're going to tell me?' she demanded when Nick did not speak. 'Do you call that an explanation? Well, I don't! It's not good enough! I——'

She broke off suddenly when she saw that Nick was not listening to her. He had leaned back against one of the units, his hands on either side of his body, resting on the worktop. The dark head was slightly bent, his eyes half closed. After a moment he sighed faintly and raised his head.

'Look,' he said, his voice slightly husky. 'I don't want to impose on you any more than I already have, but do you think I could have a coffee or something?'

The blue eyes met Erin's bewildered hazel ones as directly as before but there was something different about them now, a hazy, vaguely unfocused look that disturbed and frightened her. Studying him more closely, she saw that, underneath the tan, his face was pale and strained. There were grey shadows under his eyes and the long hands were not, as she had first thought, resting casually on the worktop but gripped the hard surface until the knuckles showed white.

'What is it?' she asked, concern combining with mistrust to make her voice sharp. 'Are you ill?'

'Not sure,' Nick's voice sounded as if it came from a long way away.

With a distinct effort he pulled himself together, shaking his head slightly as if to clear it and closing his eyes briefly as the movement jarred his cut and bruised forehead. Then the heavy eyelids lifted again and the hazy look had gone.

'Sorry about that,' he said, once more the composed, controlled man of a few moments before. 'It's just—I think it's quite a while since I had a meal.'

'Rather foolish in this weather!' Erin's response was tart, her tautly-stretched nerves giving an added edge to her voice. She had the uneasy suspicion that it was rather more than a missed meal that had had this effect on this strong-looking man. 'When did you last eat?'

Nick grinned rather shamefacedly, the smile lightening his face swiftly, and Erin registered with a shocking clarity what a devastatingly attractive man he was.

'To tell you the truth I don't know,' he admitted.

'Oh for heaven's sake!'

The exclamation escaped Erin's lips before she had time to think. The world seemed to have turned upside down and inside out. Only a short time before all she had wanted was to have this man out of her house and out of her life; now her anger seemed to have become tangled up with an exasperated concern for him. She had no doubt that Nick was not acting. The momentary faintness seemed to have passed off but his face still had that strained, shadowed look, and he was clearly making an effort just to stay on his feet. She took a deep breath before she spoke again.

'Sit down,' she instructed firmly, pulling a chair forward as she spoke.

The meekness with which he obeyed her, slumping into the chair without argument, spoke volumes for the way he was feeling. Even in their brief and unconventional acquaintance Erin had gained the impression that this Nick was not the sort of man who took orders easily. He sat silently while Erin bustled about the kitchen, moving swiftly and jerkily, as much to ease her own muddled feelings as from any need for haste. She filled the kettle and banged it down on top of the cooker with unnecessary violence.

'Do you have to make quite so much noise?' Nick asked with a hint of his earlier, sardonic tone. He was leaning his head against his hand, the long fingers resting lightly just below the bruise that was now darkening to a rather lurid purplish-red. Immediately Erin was filled with an unwilling remorse. She had completely ignored the fact that he was hurt, but then, at first, he had given no sign that the injury was troubling him.

'Does it hurt?' she asked stiffly.

'It's not comfortable,' Nick responded with what was clearly a dry understatement.

'I'd better have a look at it in a minute.'

Erin was concentrating on spooning coffee into mugs, struggling to stop her hand from shaking. In her concern for a man who was evidently unwell, she had momentarily forgotten the circumstances which had led to his being there at all but now the reality flooded back in full force and, try as she might, she could not revive the liberating feeling of anger that had driven all trace of fear from her mind. With her attention ostensibly on the drink she was preparing, she slid a covert, sidelong glance at Nick and knew that, deep down, she was desperately afraid.

Even half incapacitated-as he was, this Nick was an unnervingly forceful-looking man; a man who seemed too big in every way to be confined by the normal restrictions of ordinary life. There was a sense of controlled power about him, a restrained strength that no other man she had ever known had possessed. He seemed more at one with the wildness of the moors outside than with the cosy domesticity of the kitchen of Moor End Cottage. Briefly Erin tried to imagine what he did, where he lived, but found it impossible. There was an alien, elemental force in him that defied definition. He was a total enigma.

Dragging her thoughts back to practicalities, Erin placed the mug of coffee on the table beside Nick.

'There's sugar there if you want it,' she told him, indicating the bowl.' And I've some aspirins somewhere. A couple of them should take the edge off the pain for you.'

'Thanks,' Nick murmured briefly, curling his fingers

around the mug as if grateful for its warmth. His action
reminded Erin that he was still wearing only the thin
cotton shirt and jeans he had had on when she had
discovered him asleep on the bed. Was it only a couple
of hours ago? She had the crazy feeling she had lived
through several lifetimes since then.

'Do you have a sweater or something?' she asked
gruffly. It was not what she wanted to say but he had
looked so ill she supposed she ought to let him drink his
coffee at least before she questioned him again.

'It's with my coat I think,' Nick answered vaguely,
sipping his coffee appreciatively and seeming disinclined
to move.

'I'll get it,' Erin said hastily, glad of any excuse to get
away from his intimidating presence, if only for a few
moments. She needed time to draw breath, collect her
thoughts. 'I've got to fetch those tablets anyway.'

She fled into the living room where Nick's coat still
lay as she had first seen it, draped across the arm of the
settee. Lifting it, Erin discovered a navy blue polo-
necked sweater underneath. It was slightly damp after
lying beneath the wet jacket for so long but it would
have to do. Remembering her earlier resolution to
search Nick's coat, she hunted hastily in one pocket,
her hand closing round a packet of cigarettes and
something coldly metallic almost at once. She drew her
hand out and studied the slim metal object thoughtfully.
It was a cigarette lighter and two initials were engraved
in gold on the shiny black surface—N. H.

A man who liked to stamp his belongings with his
name, this Nick—or a man to whom people gave
expensive, personalised presents. This was no cheap,
disposable lighter and, when taken together with the
gold watch and that signet ring, it certainly did not fit
in with the idea of any common thief. Erin frowned.
Nick what? He had told her nothing beyond the fact
that his first name was Nick—and she had practically

had to force that information from him! Èven allowing
for his injury, he owed her much more than that!

Here she was, acting like a ministering angel,
making coffee, fetching painkillers—and all for a man
who had broken into her home, slept in her bed, and
was now comfortably installed in her kitchen, drinking
her coffee and looking for all the world as if he
owned the place—and all without a word of
explanation or apology!

Erin Howarth, there are times when I seriously doubt
your sanity! she told herself furiously. She was going to
have it out with him now, once and for all, she vowed,
dumping the navy jacket back on the settee with a total
indifference to the way it slid off and landed in a
crumpled heap on the floor. Never mind searching his
jacket for clues, *Nick* was the one who should tell her. It
took only a few minutes to run upstairs and fetch the
bottle of aspirins, then she headed back to the kitchen,
ready to confront Nick before her confidence evapor-
ated completely. So far he had shown no inclination
towards violence but just the same she paused before
she opened the door, her fingers tracing the narrow
outline of the knife in her pocket.

Nick was still sitting where she had left him, the
empty coffee mug beside him. He was deep in thought,
the long fingers of one hand slowly twisting the gold
signet ring round and round. At least there was one
thing she didn't have to worry about, Erin thought. He
would hardly be sitting there so calmly if anyone else
had been involved in the accident—if there had been an
accident. The release from even one of the tensions that
beset her gave her a new strength of purpose and she
marched up to the table, banging the aspirin bottle and
the cigarettes down beside his mug.

'What's the matter now?' Nick asked drily, shooting
a swift and disturbingly direct glance at Erin's flushed
face as she stood tensely on the other side of the table.

'This!' Erin declared, slamming the lighter down in front of him.

Nick reached for it infuriatingly slowly and studied it closely, turning it over and over in his hands as if he had never seen it before, a frown creasing the space between his brows.

'I don't quite see your point,' he said at last. 'It's just a cigarette lighter, rather a good one, but nothing to get worked up about.'

Erin's hands clenched against the temptation to lash out at him. He was playing with her again in the same tormenting way he had earlier—or was it a game? The frightening conviction was growing in her that for some reason he did not want her to know his name.

'What about this?' she demanded, snatching the lighter and turning it so that the initials caught the light. Her hand brushed Nick's as she did so, the first direct contact between them. The brief touch of his fingers was warm on her skin and Erin jumped as if she had been stung.

'N. H.' she said emphatically, her finger stabbing at the letters as she spoke. She was painfully aware of the way her hand and her voice shook betrayingly. 'Nick what?'

'Does it matter?' Nick asked mildly.

'Yes it does!' Erin shouted, banging her fist down on the table. 'It matters to me damn it! I want to know your name!'

'But you haven't told me yours yet,' Nick retaliated swiftly. 'And you're the one who seems to think names are so very important.'

He stood up suddenly, pushing back his chair with an abrupt movement, his action reminding Erin swiftly of just how big he was. Instinctively she took a step backwards, her eyes opening wide in panic. She was unprepared for the sudden flash of raw emotion that showed on his face, the darkening of those vivid blue eyes.

'Don't look at me like that!' Nick said, his tone rough and uneven. 'For God's sake, I'm not going to hurt you!'

'Aren't you?' Erin flung the words at him, fear making her voice high and shrill. 'Then what are you doing here? There's nothing here worth stealing!'

Nick sighed tiredly, lifting a hand to massage the muscles at the back of his neck as if to ease some intolerable tension there. His eyes looked shadowed and bleak.

'So that's what you think,' he said more quietly. 'No wonder we're talking at cross purposes; perhaps we'd better start again.'

He reached for the bottle of aspirins and shook a couple of tablets into his hand. Erin watched silently as he crossed to the sink to fill his mug with water. She had no idea what was going through his mind but she didn't trust him, not one little bit, and she refused to let herself think that he might be in pain. To do so was to risk feeling sympathy for him and she had been caught in that trap once already. The silence between them seemed to grow more oppressive with every second that passed but Erin was determined that she would not be the one to break it; Nick was the one with all the explaining to do.

'I know how it must look to you.' Nick spoke just as Erin was beginning to feel that if he did not say something soon she would scream, anything to ease the tension that was stretching every nerve in her body until she felt they might actually snap under the strain. 'But I didn't break in—though I suppose I can't blame you for suspecting I'm a thief—or a rapist. Look, what is your name?' he went on, changing the subject abruptly. 'If you don't mind telling me that is,' he added, with his sudden, disconcertingly attractive smile.

It would be easy to be disarmed by that smile, and by the quietly reasonable voice, Erin thought, striving to resist the temptation. She had to keep a clear head; this was no time to be swayed by emotion.

'It's Erin,' she said grudgingly. 'Erin Haworth,' she added, expecting him to respond with his own full name but Nick did nothing of the sort.

'Erin,' he repeated thoughtfully. 'Do you live here on your own?'

Immediately Erin stiffened, her worst suspicions and fears revived by the question and the way he had once more dodged the issue of his name.

'No I don't,' she told him coldly, crossing her fingers against the lie, praying that she sounded convincing.

'I thought not,' was Nick's response. 'A beautiful girl like you would be snapped up straight away by any man who wasn't completely blind. What's his name?'

'Who?'

Erin's response was abstracted. Had she heard right? Had he said beautiful? Was he trying a new tack, thinking he could win her round by flattery—because it wasn't going to work, she told herself firmly, ruthlessly squashing down the sudden warm glow she had felt at the casually spoken compliment.

'Your husband, or——' Nick's eyes went to Erin's left hand, lingering on the ringless third finger, 'your lover, or whatever you choose to call him.'

Erin's mind went blank. It was one thing to invent an imaginary man in order to warn this unnerving stranger to keep his distance, quite another to sustain the fiction in the face of further questioning.

'Rufus,' she said impulsively as Nick moved to pick up his sweater, her pet's name being the first that came into her head.

Nick paused for a moment and looked at her consideringly, the eyes that lingered on her face lighting with a suddenly warmly appreciative glow that roused an unwilling and unwelcome response deep inside her.

'Well tell him from me that he's a lucky man—a very lucky man indeed.'

In the few seconds it took him to pull on the navy sweater, Erin had time to wonder whether his words implied an intention to leave. She'd settle for that, she thought. What price explanations if she could just get rid of him? But Nick's next question crushed that fragile hope.

'Is he always this late?' he demanded abruptly.

Erin wetted her lips nervously, searching for the right answer. 'Sometimes,' she said carefully.

'Well I wouldn't be. The man's a fool leaving a lovely creature like you alone and unprotected in a place like this.'

'I'm quite capable of looking after myself!' Erin protested indignantly, her eyes sparkling with annoyance at his tone.

'Are you? It seems to me that you haven't got the beginnings of an idea how to cope. You neglect even the most basic rules—like locking the door after you when you go out.'

'I thought it was locked!'

Once again the situation had been turned upside down. *She* was the injured party in all this, but Nick was reproving her, criticising her negligence, and he was the last person she would have expected to do that.

'Thought isn't good enough,' Nick said inexorably. 'You should have checked. It wasn't locked and anyone could have walked in.'

'As you did!'

'As I did,' Nick agreed soberly.

'Which you still haven't explained!' Erin flashed at him in a voice that, high-pitched with nerves, did not sound at all like her own.

There it was again, that slight, questioning lift to one

dark eyebrow that somehow managed to convey so
much, implying an amused, condescending tolerance of
her impotent anger from a position of power, leaving
her in no doubt as to which of them was in control of
the situation. Erin felt she was having as much effect on
this man as a Yorkshire Terrier yapping furiously but
ineffectually at a rather lazy tiger, a tiger that was
making up its mind whether it was worth the effort of
pouncing on its prey, and the thought shattered her
precarious grip on her self-control.

'What right have you to tell me how to behave in
my own home! You walk in here without so much as a
by your leave, make yourself at home, sleep in my
bed——'

'Exactly.'

The single word broke into the flow of Erin's anger,
effectively silencing her. The cold gleam in those blue
eyes was ominously threatening and Erin's heart began
to thump painfully. Perhaps the tiger had decided to
spring after all! Not daring to take her eyes from Nick's
face, she slid her hands surreptitiously into the pocket
of her jeans, seeking the handle of the knife.

'Tell me,' Nick's voice seemed filled with silky
menace, 'would you make any man as welcome as
you've made me? Would you make him coffee, fetch an
extra blanket? Is that how you usually treat complete
strangers?'

'N—no.'

Erin's voice shook painfully. Even to herself she
could not explain the crazy impulse that had led her to
put the blanket over Nick. Now, seeing the action
through his eyes, it seemed an impossibly foolish thing
to have done.

'Then why?'

The question came with such force that Erin flinched
as if she had been struck. She recalled her earlier
determination to confront the man who had broken

into her home and force him to leave; her foolhardy
confidence then seemed laughable now. She had been
crazy to think she could have coped on her own. She
should have turned and gone straight back to the
village the minute she had found Nick's coat if not
earlier, the minute her suspicions had been aroused.
But, no she had had to stay, her stupid pride had
trapped her in this dangerous and terrifying situation.
She had been scared enough before but this coldly
angry Nick was a very different person from the man he
had seemed only minutes ago.

Now, with that moment of weakness apparently well
behind him and the thin veneer of politeness stripped
away, the full force of his physical strength came home
to Erin with a terrifying clarity. He seemed to tower
over her menacingly, seemed to fill the room so that she
was aware of nothing beyond the height and breadth of
him, the broad expanse of his chest, the powerful arms
and shoulders, and the deceptively beautiful hands that
she felt intuitively had the strength to bruise, to hurt her
with very little effort.

'Well?' Nick demanded.

'You—you said you weren't a thief or—or . . .' Erin's
voice died away, her lips would not frame the rest of the
words.

'And you believed me?' Nick's laugh was harshly
cynical. 'Dear God, what an innocent you are! Innocent
or a complete fool!'

He took a step towards her and immediately Erin
backed away hastily, coming to an abrupt halt as she
reached the wall. Nick was between her and the door,
there was nowhere she could go. Slowly, relentlessly he
came nearer, cruel blue eyes fixed on her face, clearly
noting the fear-bright eyes, the pale cheeks, the way her
breath came shallowly and unevenly. She felt sick and
faint and the knowledge of her stupidity only added to
the horror of those feelings. He had laid his trap very

carefully and subtly, lulling her into a false sense of security with his apparent lack of violence, and like a fool she had fallen straight into it. Nightmare visions of every rape or murder case she had ever read of filled her mind.

'Keep away from me!' Erin cried wildly. 'Don't touch me or I'll——'

'You'll do what, Erin?' Nick questioned softly, coming to a halt only feet away from her. 'Scratch my eyes out with those dainty little hands of yours? Or do you seriously intend using that knife you've been hiding in your pocket all this time?'

Erin's eyes opened wide in shock at his words. She could have sworn that Nick's eyes had never left her face and yet he had known—or guessed. Suddenly she was intensely grateful for the hardness of the wall at her back; without its support she felt her legs would give way beneath her. Nick took another step towards her.

'I said keep away from me!' The shrill cry echoed round the room and Nick paused, his expression thoughtful, calculating.

'All right, Erin, let's stop playing games,' he said abruptly. 'I think you've got the point,' he added, with a return to his earlier sardonic humour.

His sudden change of mood took Erin's breath away. Just what was he trying now? She stared at him numbly, seeing unbelievingly the faintest flicker of a smile on the hard line of his mouth. With a shocking gentleness he reached out a hand and touched her face, trailing the backs of his fingers lightly down her cheek.

'You couldn't use that knife you know,' he murmured softly, so seductively that Erin had to struggle to resist the hypnotic spell he was weaving.

'Couldn't I?' she spat the words at him, shaking off his hand with a brusque movement of her head. Nick's eyes gleamed with dark humour, maddening her.

'You couldn't use it,' he said firmly, reaching for her again.

Something seemed to explode in Erin's mind and, goaded beyond endurance, she closed her fingers around the wooden handle of the knife, tugging at it frantically, trying to get it free.

'Erin!' Nick's voice held a note of warning, one she was beyond heeding. A final pull and the knife was out of her pocket and she held it up between them, the point towards Nick's chest.

'I told you not to touch me,' she said jerkily, a glorious sense of triumph filling her as she saw the way he hesitated then drew back ever so slightly.

But her triumph was pitifully short-lived. Nick's reactions were lightning-swift, his speed amazing for such a big man. There was a blur of movement, a sudden agonising pain in her right wrist, and a noisy clatter as the knife flew from her nerveless fingers and hit a cupboard on the opposite side of the room. Then she was slammed back against the wall, her arm twisted up behind her so that she feared she would break it if she tried to move. In a blind panic she lifted her free hand to strike out at Nick only to find that captured too and forced impotently down to her side.

'Keep still, damn you!' She heard Nick's voice in her ear, scarcely penetrating the red haze that filled her mind. 'Erin, keep still, I don't want to hurt you!'

She could feel the hard strength of his body against her own, pinning her against the wall, and realised the futility of trying to escape; to fight would only anger him, make him hurt her more. As her struggles slowed, Nick loosened his grip, not releasing her but holding her easily, knowing his own strength and using it to keep her where he wanted until he was ready to let go.

At last, when she stood silent and shaking, he turned her slowly to face him, placing one hand on either side of her body, imprisoning her. Fearfully Erin raised her eyes to his face then immediately looked away again, the stony, implacable set of his features terrifying her.

'Now,' Nick said grimly, 'perhaps you'll listen to me.'

At that moment the lights flickered and went out.

CHAPTER THREE

'NICK!'

Erin's involuntary cry of panic, the cry of a terrified, bewildered child, echoed eerily in the blackness. It was as if someone had suddenly flung a blanket over her head; she could almost feel the weight of the darkness pressing down on her and she could see nothing though she strained her eyes until they ached. Fear closed her throat so that she thought she would choke. She could see nothing, hear nothing. It was as if all her senses had suddenly ceased to function and she was shiveringly cold.

Gropingly she reached out a hand to where Nick had been just in front of her but her fingers touched only empty air. Instinctively she choked back the sound that rose to her lips, every nerve alert to any sound or movement that might tell her just where her unknown tormentor might be. Had he gone, escaped under cover of darkness? Or was he still there, hidden, waiting? She didn't know which was worse—to be alone, blind and frightened in this house that no longer seemed like a home to her, or to know that somewhere in the room Nick stood silently, waiting for her to make a move.

In the dark like this she was so much more vulnerable, completely at the mercy of a man who had terrified her only moments before—and yet in the second she had reached out and found him gone she had felt not relief but a sharp sense of loss.

Erin dug her nails into her palms, the small, sharp pain clearing her mind, bringing back a sense of reality. The sudden descent of the darkness had been the last straw, destroying her self-control, and in a childish reaction to her fear she had called out to the only other human being near her—which was the worst thing she could have done. What she should have done was to use the slight advantage the black-out gave her. She knew the house, Nick did not. Her bedroom door had a lock on it. If she could find her way there, she could bar the door against him.

But where was Nick? Was he still between her and the door? If she moved would she blunder straight into him? If only he would speak or make some sound!

Painfully slowly Erin inched forward, heading for where she believed the door to be, her ears straining for the faintest sound. Nothing. Perhaps he had gone after all. The thought made her over-confident and she took a foolishly hasty step forward, banging awkwardly into hard wood as she came up against the table, its corner jabbing agonisingly into her thigh, bringing tears to her eyes so that she could not hold back a cry of pain and despair.

'It's all right, Erin, I'm here.'

Nick's voice came quietly, shockingly close by, making her heart beat so fiercely in panic that its thudding against her chest almost drowned the sound of the wind outside. But it was the soothing, almost gentle note in it that rocked Erin's sense of reality. She froze where she stood, praying that if she didn't make a sound he wouldn't be able to judge where she was.

Nick moved at last and now Erin thought she saw him vaguely, a darker, more substantial shadow in the gloom, and unnervingly near. She wanted to run but the terror that had returned with the destruction of her fragile hope that he might have gone paralysed her, and the dull ache in her leg was a painful reminder of the failure of her last attempt at escape.

'Erin?' Nick's voice was softly questioning.

Erin started violently as she felt his hand on her arm, very lightly; it would be easy to break free but still she couldn't move. Then his fingers touched her cheek and she heard his muttered curse as he felt the wetness of her tears against his skin.

'Erin!' he said again in shock and disbelief and to her horror his arms came round her, making her heart seem to stop then jolt back into action again so fiercely that she could hardly breathe. 'Dear child, it's only a power cut. The snow's probably brought the lines down somewhere. There's nothing to be afraid of.'

There's you! Erin wanted to scream but she couldn't voice the words because her throat had closed up in panic. The shock of his sudden gentleness drove all thought from her mind but underneath the fear was a new and intensely disturbing realisation. She felt the warmth of Nick's arms with an added sensitivity because she could not see and, unbelicvably, shockingly, she *wanted* the comfort of that warmth, wanted it in a way that had nothing to do with any fear of the dark.

Her hands came up to push desperately at Nick's chest expecting his grip to tighten but, incredibly, Nick released her at once without any attempt to restrain her.

'It's not just the dark, is it?' Nick's quietly spoken words startled Erin, coming so close to her own secret thoughts. She tensed ready for flight, common sense warring with a more basic, primitive need.

Every instinct she possessed should have been screaming at her to get away, telling her she had much more to fear from Nick himself than any minor upset caused by the loss of the electricity supply, but crazily, impossibly, they were telling her exactly the opposite. She had felt safe in Nick's arms, unbelievably so.

'I never meant things to go that far,' Nick murmured in a voice that was very faintly unsteady. 'I just wanted to make you think. You were so defenceless, so vulnerable, and too bloody trusting for your own good. You should have called the police or, at the very least, turfed me out of that bed the minute you found me.

Instead you tuck me in all warm and cosy in some crazy maternalistic gesture. You can't imagine how I felt when I woke up and found that blanket over me! Then you rush around finding aspirins, fetching my sweater so I don't feel cold——'

'You were ill!' Erin protested defensively, thoroughly confused by the sudden change from the dark tormentor to someone who was actually *reproving* her for helping him.

'Maybe I was,' Nick agreed seriously. 'But are you going to offer a home to every stray dog that wanders into your house? Because I warn you, Erin, one of these days some vicious little stray is going to turn round and bite you if you're not very careful.'

'You needed help.' Erin's voice was very low. She winced as Nick's hand gripped her arm bruisingly.

'What do I have to do to make you see!' He sighed his exasperation. 'Erin, my sweet innocent, you don't know me! You know nothing about me! Why *didn't* you call the police when you found me? Why don't you do it now?'

The rational, sane half of Erin's mind told her that the worst thing she could possibly do was to reveal to Nick that she hadn't even got a phone while the other, more emotional half was whispering that if he was telling her to call the police then he could have nothing to fear if she did—and she was quite unprepared for the dizzying sense of release that thought brought her.

'You can't mean that!' she exclaimed, trying vainly to see some expression on the dark blur of his face above her.

'Can't I? Erin, it's what I expected. When I woke up in that room I fully believed I would find the police waiting for me at the foot of the stairs. I could have handled that. Instead I find you—and, dammit, I'm not at all sure I know how to handle you!'

Erin was suddenly intensely grateful for the darkness

that hid the bewilderment, the mass of confused emotions she knew must be written on her face. She could not believe that this Nick was the same man who had driven her to pull a knife on him. It was as if, since the time he had first appeared in the kitchen, Nick had been three completely different people, each of them disturbingly dangerous in their own way, and she was not at all sure which one of them presented the greatest threat.

What *was* she doing? *Why* wasn't she fighting Nick— or at least making some effort to get away? Because she didn't want to. The answer came with a shocking certainty, making her feel cold all over. It was wrong, it was stupid, but she was drawn to Nick, drawn to the comfort of his nearness like some small, frightened animal seeking refuge.

But Nick meant danger, not safety. And yet there had been that moment, just after he had knocked the knife from her hand, when he had said he didn't want to hurt her. He'd said it earlier too, she remembered— could she trust that now?

This must be how it felt to be blind, she thought, the loss of one sense bringing with it a heightened awareness of all the others. She could hear the soft sound of Nick's breathing, she could scent very faintly the subtle tange of aftershave mixed with a more potent, essentially masculine aroma that set her nerves quivering in a way that was quite unlike the terror of moments before and yet was very much the same.

'I think you're managing pretty well,' she said huskily then cried out sharply as his hands closed over her shoulders, hard fingers digging into tender flesh, hurting as she had known they could, and yet somehow the pain did not matter.

'Erin!' Nick protested and the word was neither a laugh nor a groan but something between the two. 'You haven't listened to a word I've said. You make me wish

I'd left here as soon as I woke up—which was what I planned to do. And I would have done too if I hadn't been curious to discover just who'd put that damn blanket over me. It would have been better if I'd gone,' he went on almost to himself. 'I should never have stayed—I should go now.'

Gently he eased away from Erin and without the warmth of his body close to her she felt suddenly bereft, alone in a way she had never known before. It was as if the now unseen world had ceased to exist and there were only the two of them. Nick's strength was the only real, tangible thing in the darkness that surrounded them and she needed that strength, needed it now. He had told her to call the police, showing no fear of what would happen if she did, had been about to go without harming her or her home, and for now that was enough.

'Nick, no!' she cried sharply, catching hold of his arm.

Nick made a move as if to shake off her hand then stilled suddenly, waiting.

'Please stay,' Erin pleaded. 'Just until the power's restored—please!'

'And what about this man of yours, this Rufus?' Nick's voice sounded stiff and tight. 'What if he came back and I was here?'

Erin did not hesitate. If there had been any glimmer of light, if she could have seen Nick's face or he hers, she doubted if she would have been able to tell him, but in the blinding darkness she felt she could say anything.

'He doesn't exist,' she said firmly. 'I made him up.'

For a moment she thought Nick had not heard her. If it had not been for the hardness and warmth beneath her fingers she might almost have believed he had gone already, he was so still and silent. The newly heightened sensitivity her temporary blindness had brought continued to work on her so that she was disturbingly aware of the warmth of his body beneath the soft wool of his sleeve and felt the muscles in his arm tense as he began to pull away from her, but then he paused and turned back again. Erin found she could hardly breathe, she wished desperately that she could see his face.

'Just until the lights come on again,' Nick said slowly. 'Just that—and then I go.'

'Just that,' Erin echoed softly, quite unprepared for the bubble of happiness that had nothing to do with relief that rose up inside her, making her feel strangely light-headed. Impulsively she reached for Nick and gave him a quick, warm hug of gratitude.

She had fully intended that that would be all, that then she would move away again, but Nick's arms came round her swiftly in response, pinning her close up against him, his fingers spreading out across her back, tracing soft, enticing patterns up and down her spine. His touch was light at first but then the pressure increased subtly in a way that forced a murmur of response from Erin's lips as she felt Nick's mouth on her hair, drifting brief, tantalising kisses across its softness.

'Nick!' Erin whispered his name but whether in protest or encouragement even she could not tell.

Acting on some instinct that went deeper than rational thought, Erin lifted her face at exactly the moment that Nick's head, invisible in the darkness, lowered towards hers and their lips met unerringly with an inevitability that was as natural as breathing.

Nick's kiss was warm and soft, as gentle as the hands that were sliding across her shoulders to caress her neck beneath the fall of golden brown hair. Erin leaned her head back against those hands, glorying in the feel of their strength, a strength no longer used to hurt but to please, holding her possessively so that she could not have moved away even if she had wanted to.

But she knew she had no desire to draw away. She

met Nick more than half-way, returning his kiss willingly, her lips parting under his, her body softly pliant against his hardness. Her hands strayed over the powerful lines of his back and shoulders, finally tangling in the dark softness of his hair. Nick was whispering her name against her skin as his lips brushed her forehead, her eyelids, and then came back to her mouth.

'This is madness,' he groaned softly and Erin sighed a faint, wordless sound of agreement. If this was madness, she prayed she might never return to sanity.

She did not know if seconds or an eternity had passed, had no idea if some sound from outside had broken in on the tiny, magical world they had created, but suddenly, with shattering abruptness, Nick's mood had changed. His hands closed around her arms with a new and very different touch, controlled, impersonal, distancing her from him more effectively than his brusque movement away from her side.

'What the hell are you doing to me?' he demanded harshly. 'Erin, this has got to stop right now!'

He released her abruptly and she felt him turn away, hunting for something in the darkness. Then the lighter flared briefly as he lit a cigarette and in the faint, unsteady glow of the flame Erin saw his face, shadowed and hard, the face of a stranger, before the darkness descended once more.

With half her mind Erin registered the fact that Nick was swearing steadily and savagely but whether at her, at himself, or simply at the restrictions imposed on him by the power failure she did not know and she could not begin to think clearly enough to consider the question properly. She felt as if the all-pervading blackness had filled her mind; if she had been lonely and frightened before it was as nothing when compared with the way she felt now. But far worse than the loneliness and the fear was the fact that she did not understand. She could make no sense of Nick's

behaviour, his sudden changes of mood; she did not
know why he was here or what he planned to do; and,
worst of all, she did not understand herself.

How could she have let this man, a frightening,
threatening stranger, hold her and kiss her like that?
But it had been all she had wanted! She had gone into
his arms as willingly as if she had known him almost all
her life—as she had known Geoff. Erin flinched; she did
not want to think of Geoff. Only a few weeks before she
had stood in Bradwood Parish Church, an unwilling
guest at Becky and Geoff's wedding, and thought that
her heart was dead, that she would never feel anything
for any man again. But she had not thought of Geoff
when she was in Nick's arms, indeed she had not
thought at all but had simply responded, her body
finely tuned to his so that when he had put her from
him she had been devastated, lost and alone in a world
turned suddenly cold and alien, a world in which the
rules by which she lived no longer applied if a man she
did not know, a man she feared, could have this effect
on her.

She and Geoff had never been lovers; Erin had
never felt ready for that sort of commitment. She had
enjoyed being in his arms, had welcomed the warm,
secure feeling his kisses and the restrained caresses
that had been their only physical lovemaking had
brought her, but she had never known how it felt to
want his love so desperately that all other consider-
ations were forgotten.

Nick had done no more than kiss her. He had made
no attempt to seduce her, had hardly touched her and
yet her body was burning hot, glowing as if he had
actually made love to her. There had been no security in
his kisses but they had woken a physical longing in her
that all Geoff's caresses had failed to arouse. She felt
strangely fulfilled yet deeply dissatisfied. She had
wanted more, much more than he had given.

Dimly Erin became aware that Nick had spoken to her and she had not heard a word he said.

'I'm sorry,' she said jerkily, shaking her head to clear her whirling thoughts. 'What did you say?'

'We need some light.' Nick sounded impatient. 'You must have a torch—or candles.'

It took only a few minutes to find and light the small supply of candles and soon a soft glow lifted the heavy curtain of darkness. But as the gloom vanished so did the strange intimacy they had shared and Nick was once more the disturbing, enigmatic stranger, his carefully controlled manner covering every trace of the man who had held her in his arms. Reaction making her weak, Erin leaned back against the cooker then jerked away again as she felt its heat.

'Are you hungry?' she asked impulsively, speaking to fill the silence, a silence that seemed filled with the questions she had not got the courage to ask. 'I made a casserole, it should be ready by now.'

'You have it.' Nick was lighting another candle as he spoke, his eyes fixed on the flame. 'I can't take your food.'

'But you said you hadn't eaten for ages!' Erin protested, mentally registering his refusal as another point in his favour. 'And I think there's enough for two.'

Nick's head swung round at her words and he studied her intently for a long moment, his eyes darkly unfathomable in the candlelight so that Erin held her breath, her stomach clenching nervously. Then, unexpectedly, he laughed, dispelling the uneasy tension that had seemed almost tangible between them.

'Erin Howarth, you are incorrigible!' he exclaimed, a smile tugging at the corners of his mouth. 'After all I've said, you're still fussing round me like a mother hen. You really are one crazy lady!'

'Well you don't look as if you've been taking care of

yourself!' Erin declared, encouraged by the lighter, teasing quality in his voice and cravenly shelving the questions that were still unanswered, wanting to keep the new peace between them for just a little longer. 'You're far too thin for one thing—you look as if you haven't had a square meal in weeks.'

Abruptly Nick's mood sobered, the smile fading swiftly from his face.

'I suspect I have to plead guilty, milady,' he said flatly, not meeting her eyes.

He remained silent for a moment, apparently absorbed in his thoughts, troublesome, unwelcome thoughts to judge from the frown that clouded his face. Then he flexed his shoulders tiredly, forcing a smile.

'So if you're serious about that offer of a meal, I'm not even going to try to refuse,' he said, his light tone almost but not quite disguising the darker, harder edge to his voice.

'We'll eat in the living room.' Erin was relieved to find she sounded much more confident than she actually felt. 'There's a fire in there, it'll be much warmer than this ice-box.'

And when we've eaten, she vowed, I'm going to find out all about you—and you're not going to put me off this time.

It was not the easiest of meals. Erin was too much on edge to taste the food she chewed and swallowed automatically, her mind whirling with disordered, disjointed thoughts. Who *was* Nick? And what hidden reason had he for not giving his name? She knew she hadn't handled their meeting as well as she might have done but it wasn't just her own nervous bungling of the situation that had resulted in her being no wiser now than when he had first appeared in the kitchen. Each time she had come close to finding out something Nick had jumped, sending the conversation off at a tangent, and she had been fool enough to let herself be distracted by his questions, his apparent concern for her safety—a concern that could all too easily be assumed. She had been diverted from her original line of thought before she had quite realised it had been done. Now her mind reeled in dread at the thought of what he might be hiding from her.

Her eyes slid to the dark figure on the opposite side of the fireplace, her tension growing as she saw the preoccupied frown on Nick's face. In spite of the fact that he had admitted to not having had a meal for some time he had eaten very little, barely touching the food on his plate. Erin's heart sank as she saw that the closed, shuttered look she had already come to dread was back in place once more. She could never have let *this* man kiss her, she thought, then her heart lurched violently at the realisation of her own foolishness. This man was Nick; she had seen this side of him before—but she had still wanted him to kiss her so much that she had thought she would go mad if he did not.

Suddenly there was a rustle of movement from the depths of the settee and a sleek, sinuous shape slid from the cushions, landing on the floor with a soft thud. Immediately Nick swung round, tensing instinctively.

'What the hell was that?'

There was no way Erin could control the near-hysterical laughter that rose up inside her. After spending so long with her nerves stretched tight she felt she had either to laugh or to scream and Nick's bewildered expression was all that it took to spark off a fit of giggles that shook her helplessly.

'Erin?' Nick questioned sharply as she collapsed back in her chair. 'Erin, what——'

'Rufus,' Erin gasped unevenly. 'That was Rufus.'

'Rufus? But you said——'

Nick glanced towards the door just in time to see the

tip of a tail disappearing behind it. The look on his face brought Erin's giggles back in full force.

'You asked if I lived here on my own,' she managed eventually. 'So I told you the truth; I said I shared the cottage with someone called Rufus.'

'But you carefully neglected to mention that Rufus was a cat!' Nick's tone was indignant but Erin was relieved to see that a smile had wiped the shuttered look from his face. This time she did not question the heady sensation of happiness that swept through her but simply let it happen until her mood was changed swiftly as all colour faded suddenly from Nick's face and he lifted a hand to the disfiguring bruise on his forehead.

'I ought to have a look at that,' she said hastily. 'Does it hurt very much?'

'I'll live,' was Nick's dry response. 'But I suppose it would do no harm to clean it up a bit. The cut's not very deep,' he added reassuringly. 'It's the bruising that makes it look worse than it is.'

'It is pretty spectacular,' Erin agreed, not entirely convinced. How would she cope if he was ill? She didn't even know how he'd been injured. 'How did it happen?'

The impulsive words slipped out and as soon as they had Erin bit her lip hard, wishing them back again, terrified that she had spoken too soon, blurting the question out without thought. She nerved herself, waiting for the explosion. It didn't come. Nick's expression was thoughtful but not hostile as he pushed his plate away and reached for his cigarettes, lighting one and drawing on it deeply before he spoke.

'It's all right, Erin,' he said at last, 'I'm not about to bite your head off, if that's what's worrying you. As a matter of fact I was about to bring up the subject myself. I'm well aware that I owe you an explanation—you've been remarkably patient, not pushing me for one, but I can't let things go on like this—I have to tell you as much as I know.'

Erin knew her confusion must show in her face but she made no attempt to try and disguise it. She was struggling to grasp what Nick was saying but the words seemed to slide about in her head, slipping out of reach as soon as she tried to get a grip on them, and Nick's expression gave her no help at all. He was sitting well back in his chair, his dark hair blending with the gloom around him. The shifting, flickering firelight barely illuminated his face, throwing disturbing shadows around his eyes, deepening the harsh lines of his face. Suddenly she found that she had been holding her breath and she let it go in a long, bewildered sigh.

'You're not making any sense,' she said slowly. 'I don't understand.' Her voice sharpened as she spoke. 'I don't know what you're playing at, but I wish you'd stop it!'

'Erin, for God's sake don't make this more difficult than it is!' Nick sat up suddenly, flinging his cigarette into the fire with a violent movement. 'I'm not playing with you, I'm trying to tell you, but there isn't very much I can say.'

He rubbed the back of his hand across his eyes in a gesture of weariness and confusion then turned to stare deep into the heart of the fire as if seeking inspiration. Erin suddenly felt icy cold. What was it Nick was so reluctant to tell her? All at once she wished the last few minutes had never been, that she had never asked that impulsive question. It was sheer cowardice, she knew, but she wanted to go back to the sort of peace there had been before.

Nick seemed to have come to a decision. He turned back to Erin and she shivered when she saw the bleakness of his eyes. She didn't want to know!

'Nick——' she began nervously but the words died

on her lips at the look on his face. She froze, waiting.

'I can't remember,' Nick said harshly, his words falling starkly into the silence.

CHAPTER FOUR

FOOLISHLY, Erin's first reaction was one of overwhelming relief. She had imagined so many things in the few seconds before Nick spoke, dreadful, frightening things that had driven her nearly distracted just to think of them, that the truth seemed almost comforting by comparison. Nick's words had explained so many mysteries—the strange business with the watch, the frequent, swift changing of the subject when questioned about his identity—everything now slipped into place like the final pieces of a jigsaw puzzle, completing the picture.

Is that all! She almost said the words out loud then froze as the full implications of what he had said came home to her with a force that made her head reel.

What Nick had told her altered everything and yet it changed nothing at all. She still did not know who he was, still had no idea whether he had entered her home intent on theft or assault. He could be anyone—a murderer, a terrorist—and she would never know and Nick could not help her either. His past was as much a mystery to him as it was to her if—and here was the most worrying thought of all—if he was even telling her the truth.

'Frightening, isn't it?'

Nick's voice broke in on Erin's thoughts. He had been watching her silently, noting the swift play of emotions across her face. Erin seriously wondered if he had the ability to read her thoughts; his gaze was so intent and probing she might almost have believed he could.

'But what happened? Were you in an accident? Was anyone else hurt?'

Nick shook his dark head confusedly.

'Do you think I haven't asked myself all that?'

'Don't you remember anything?'

'Little enough,' was the laconic response in a voice that was only very faintly unsteady. 'I remember lying in the snow. I must have fallen—that's probably when I got this.' He touched his forehead briefly. 'Perhaps I'd been unconscious for some time, I don't know—and I don't *think* anyone was with me—certainly I was alone when I woke up. After that I walked for what seemed like hours; I didn't know where I was going, I just knew I had to keep going. Then I saw a house—this house— the curtains weren't drawn and I could see the fire so I knew the place was inhabited; I didn't mean to barge in uninvited.'

Nick shot a rueful, apologetic glance in Erin's direction and she coloured slightly at the memory of her own angry words. Nick's emotionless recounting of events as if they had happened to someone else, not to him, and the hint of teasing humour at the end bewildered her. How could he joke about something like this? Then, meeting his eyes at last, she saw the dark flame burning in them and recognised the unnatural control for what it was—an inhuman effort to impose order on the unbearable. Surely he couldn't fake that?

'And that's all? You can't remember anything else?'

Nick frowned, staring into the darkness.

'I did knock,' he said slowly, 'but there was no answer. I don't know what made me try the door—I was desperate I suppose, I would have tried anything. I couldn't believe my luck when it actually opened. I'm not quite sure what I did then—the next thing I remember is waking up in that bed upstairs——' He stopped abruptly, his hands clenching tightly as if to grasp some elusive memory. 'I had a bag,' he said suddenly. 'I was carrying a bag. Did I bring it in with me?'

'There was no bag here,' Erin told him quietly. 'What was it like?'

Nick closed his eyes trying to visualise the scene in his mind, his concentration so intense it almost hurt to witness it.

'Black, I think, and leather—not a suitcase, just the sort of thing you'd take if you were going away for a weekend.' He shook his head despondently. 'Not much to go on, is it?'

'But it's something,' Erin declared, praying she sounded more confident than she felt. 'For one thing, if there was someone else and they were hurt you'd be unlikely to pick up your bag and walk away—you'd want to get help as quickly as possible so you wouldn't want to be burdened by luggage.'

'But I don't *know* that!' The rigid control had slipped momentarily and that was so disturbing that it sent Erin searching through everything Nick had said because there had been something else, something very slight—but important.

'You said you woke up lying in the snow—that you'd fallen and hit your head—so there was no car accident or anything, nothing that anyone else could have been involved in. You didn't see a car, did you?'

Nick shook his head slowly. His eyes looked bruised and dazed and Erin shivered at the realisation that she was the one who was thinking clearly enough to be in control of the situation. It was an awesome responsibility, one she was not at all sure she could handle.

'There must be some way you can find out more. What about your jacket? There could be a wallet or something.'

She made a move to fetch the coat from the settee but Nick was there before her, bringing it back to the light of the fire as he hunted through the pockets. Erin kept her eyes fixed on his hands, not wanting to see the expression on his face. On the second attempt she saw the tension in his body as his hand touched something. Without speaking he withdrew his hand and held it out. In his palm, glinting softly in the firelight, lay a set of car keys.

'So there was a car,' Nick said slowly. 'But I wouldn't just lock the door on someone who was hurt, pocket the keys and walk off—I couldn't.' It was a statement, not a question, but a doubtful, hesitant note in his voice left Erin with the certainty that he was testing his own feelings.

With a sudden angry movement Nick clenched his fingers over the keys.

'God, I wish these lights would come back on!'

Something twisted in Erin's heart at his words. She could understand his impatience, the almost overpowering need to be doing something, anything that would help him discover who he was, but was that all? Was he anxious to see the power restored so that he was freed from his promise to stay with her? There was no reason why that should hurt so much; Erin only knew that it did.

'I'm going to look for that bag,' Nick announced abruptly, making a move as if to get to his feet. The pallor of his face shocked Erin into action.

'Oh no you're not!' she declared, moving in front of his chair, blocking his way. 'You're going nowhere until I've seen to that cut.'

'Erin, don't fuss!' Nick snapped irritably. 'I've had a bang on the head, that's all. I've survived worse—or, rather,' he amended wryly, 'I *think* I've survived worse.'

But Erin was not to be swayed. The attempt at humour had not deceived her, Nick's expression was far from humorous, and while he was sitting down she was, temporarily at least, in control—though she didn't fancy her chances if he tried to resist her.

'Nick, don't be an idiot,' she said as forcefully as she

dared. 'That cut should have been cleaned up hours ago, and what you've just told me makes it rather more than just a bang on the head—you've lost your memory for heaven's sake!'

'I don't need reminding of that fact,' Nick growled, but Erin was relieved to see that he sat back in his chair, apparently abandoning his intention to hunt for the missing bag and, as before, the sudden and uncharacteristic meekness with which he submitted told her much more than anything he said.

'I'll get some hot water and antiseptic,' she told him briskly. 'And don't move!'

'Yes, nurse!' Nick's response had a flash of humour but there was not even the hint of a smile on his face as he spoke.

Erin half suspected that when she returned to the living room she would find that Nick had disobeyed her instructions and got up, but he was sitting exactly where she had left him, staring blindly into the darkness. His face looked drawn and pale and his shoulders slumped tiredly as if, as soon as she was out of the room, he had abandoned what she now realised was a careful act he had been putting on for her benefit and admitted to the weakness he had refused to show until now.

'Nick!' The shocked exclamation was only a whisper but Nick heard it and his head jerked round swiftly.

With an effort that was frightening in a man who had earlier seemed so strong, so in control, he straightened his shoulders and forced a smile; a smile that was supposed to be reassuring but which in fact had quite the opposite effect. Erin saw the bleakness of Nick's eyes, the way the smile did not touch them at all and she was suddenly very much afraid—but afraid *for* Nick rather than of him and that made it so much harder to cope with.

'I've brought some more aspirins,' she said hastily, thrusting the tablets at him awkwardly as she struggled to assume a calm and confident expression. It would do no good if she let her fears show now. The situation had been turned upside down and *she* had to be the strong one. 'If you lean your head on the back of the chair and I put a candle here I should be able to see what I'm doing.'

Erin was moving the candle as she spoke, unable to look at Nick, wanting to give him time, feeling instinctively that he would hate it if he knew she had seen through the careful act he was determined was all she should see. Compliant as a tired child, Nick let his head drop back against the chair.

'I can see I'm not going to get any peace until you've done your Florence Nightingale bit,' he said resignedly, his tone bringing an involuntary smile to Erin's lips. This was more like the Nick she knew.

She dipped some cotton wool into the bowl of warm water then paused uncertainly, strangely reluctant to touch him. Her hands felt suddenly clumsy and she was very much afraid of hurting Nick, but there was something else, something that swept away all her former resolve leaving her confused and unsure.

'Well, go on,' Nick said sharply, jolting her into action.

The cut on Nick's head looked even more ugly and painful close to and, as she bathed it gently, wiping away the dried blood, all her nervousness vanished as swiftly as it had come, driven from her mind by a tide of concern for him. Nick lay passive under her hands, his eyes closed, his apparent docility every bit as unnerving as his earlier, more hostile mood, and Erin frowned in distress as she felt the hot, bruised skin beneath her fingers. The dark hair had fallen forward on to Nick's forehead, getting in her way, so that she brushed it aside lightly, and a tingling sensation strangely like an electric shock ran up her arm as she felt its silky softness. Standing behind him, looking

down at his shadowed face, she was intensely aware of
the broad cheekbones, the way the long lashes lay like
dark crescents against the tanned skin, and she had to
pause to collect her thoughts, her hands noticeably
unsteady, before she could return to her task.

Nick had been right, the wound was not deep. With
luck it would heal fairly quickly and once the bruising
had gone the thin, jagged line would hardly be
noticeable. If only his mind would heal as quickly! Erin
had never felt so completely helpless, she knew nothing
at all about amnesia and had no idea what to do for the
best.

'You should have a doctor look at this,' she said
worriedly. 'Concussion can be pretty nasty and I really
don't know what to do. I wish I had a phone then at
least we could get some advice.'

Nick's eyes flew open, looking straight up into Erin's
face, and the colour fled from her face as she realised
just what she had given away.

'So that's why you didn't contact the police!' he said
almost angrily, and she could see that he was thinking
back over the evening, remembering things she had
said.

'It wasn't just that!' Erin protested. 'I . . .'

Her voice died away. How could she explain an
instinct? How could she put into words that irrational,
inexplicable feeling of sympathy she had felt when she
had heard him talk in his sleep? The sensation had been
so fleeting and so sharp that it had coloured her
reactions to Nick ever since.

'I wonder if I'll ever understand you,' Nick
murmured softly.

He reached up and took hold of Erin's hand where it
rested on the back of the chair, just above his shoulder.

'You're one hell of a lady,' he went on thoughtfully,
his long fingers idly tracing gentle patterns across the
back of her hand. 'Quite unique.'

'No I'm not!'

Erin's protest came shakily. Nick's touch, light as it was, was doing strange things to her heart, making it race in a way that left her feeling breathless, a sensation which was made all the more disconcerting by the knowledge that it was quite irrational—and dangerously so.

'You can't say that,' she said sharply. 'You don't know of anyone you can compare me with; if you did you'd see that I'm very ordinary and—'

She broke off in consternation as she made a move to pull her hand away and Nick's grip tightened suddenly. Slowly and irresistibly he drew her hand towards him so that she was forced to move round to the side of the chair and then, when Nick still did not release her, had to kneel on the floor beside him, her hand still held captive between both of his. Very slowly and emphatically Nick shook his head.

'Not ordinary,' he said, his eyes fixed on Erin's hand. 'Never that. Right now I'd be willing to bet that you're the most extraordinary lady I've ever met.'

Without warning he lifted Erin's hand to his lips and pressed a kiss against it, folding her fingers down over her palm and holding them firmly as if to keep the caress imprisoned there.

'Nick, please—' Erin said huskily then hesitated, not knowing how to continue. Besides, she didn't quite trust her voice; it seemed strangely weak and unreliable.

'Nick, please—' Nick mimicked softly. 'Please what, Erin?' he added, the vivid blue eyes suddenly swinging round to her. 'Please yes or please no? I want to kiss you,' he went on, his voice suddenly soft and enticing. 'The question is, will you let me?'

Erin could not answer him; how could she when she did not know what she wanted to say? Her throat was very dry and tight and she very much suspected that if she tried to speak her voice would fail her completely.

She knew she should say no, knew how dangerous it was to say yes, and she didn't want to say either word.

Nick had released her hand but Erin did not move though he held her still only by the hypnotic force of his intent blue gaze. Erin had the craziest feeling that her mind was no longer in her body but suspended far above it, watching through a whirling haze as Nick leaned towards her; every action seeming to be performed in slow motion.

Erin accepted his kiss passively, the drowsy, unreal feeling that filled her drugging her brain, leaving it incapable of thought. Her body felt heavy, languorous, and yet she seemed to be floating, her head swimming so that she closed her eyes against the sudden, crazy tilting of the room as if the world had swung round her. She swayed weakly and felt the strength of Nick's arms come round her, holding her upright and drawing her towards him and she knew that without their support she would have fallen.

'What are you?' Nick murmured, punctuating his words with slow, soft kisses across Erin's face. 'Some sort of enchantress? I'd swear you'd bewitched me. I don't know who the hell I am, and I'm damn sure I'll regret this in the morning, but somehow that doesn't matter. Right now, nothing matters but the fact that you're here in my arms and—Oh God, Erin!'

Nick's hands clenched tightly in her hair and the dark head bent, his mouth coming down on hers. There was no gentleness now, only a fierce passion that forced her lips open, crushing them bruisingly, smothering her involuntary cry of pain. The languid, unreal feeling vanished, swept away on a tidal wave of sensation that cleared the haze from Erin's mind, replacing it with a new and heightened awareness of her own body and Nick's and the fire they had lit between them.

No longer content to remain passive in Nick's arms, she reached for him, wanting desperately to touch him.

Impatiently she pushed at his sweater, sliding her hands under the dark wool to tug at the buttons of his shirt, a sigh of contentment escaping her only when she felt the smooth warmth of his skin beneath her fingertips. Her touch stilled Nick suddenly and he lifted his head slightly, the blue eyes touched with a hint of the wary, guarded look that had filled them earlier. But Erin was beyond caring what he was thinking; she didn't want him to think, she wanted him to kiss her again so that she could recapture the heart-stopping pleasure that had coursed through her a moment before.

Kiss me! a small, insistent voice was whispering feverishly inside her head. Please, please, kiss me!

She didn't know whether she had spoken the words out loud or if Nick simply responded to the invitation in her eyes but she had her wish and a soft, exultant laugh escaped her as she felt his lips on her throat, trailing kisses up towards the corner of her mouth.

Without being aware that he had moved, she found that Nick was beside her, easing her slowly backwards until she lay on the rug, bathed in the warmth of the fire. But the glow that filled her as Nick stretched himself out beside her, gathering her close in his arms, had nothing to do with the brightly burning flames but came from deep within her. She felt as if her need of Nick was burning her up like a fever so that the brief, beguiling kisses he dropped on her face and hair were not enough to satisfy, serving only to inflame the longing that was pervading her. She wanted more! She needed to know that the yearning aching she felt was mutual, that the passion he had aroused in her had touched him too.

Blindly she wrapped her arms around Nick, pulling him down to her so that he lay half across her, imprisoning her with the hard weight of his body. Now she was kissing him, abandoning all pretence of restraint, not caring what he might think of her eager surrender, the mute invitation of her body. She made no protest when Nick's hands eased off her sweater and found the buttons on her shirt but lay trembling with anticipation, longing for the touch of his fingers on her heated flesh.

The cry that broke from her when his hand finally closed over her breast after what seemed like an eternity of waiting was a sound of wonder, an instinctive, primitive moan that faded to a gasp of pure happiness. The long fingers moved softly over her delicate skin, teasing, arousing, bringing a throbbing pleasure that pounded through her body, blotting out all thought beyond the need to touch Nick, hold him so closely, become a part of him because only with him could she be complete. She heard a voice that did not sound like her own call his name as the pressure of his hands increased and her own fingers clenched convulsively on his shoulders, digging into the powerful muscles as she clung to him, murmuring her need incoherently.

'God in heaven!'

The muffled curse jarred on Erin's nerves, reaching her even through the delirium that filled her mind. Nick moved away so suddenly that for a moment she was not aware that he had gone. Her hands still reached out for him, she even arched her body slightly, thinking to find him just inches away, before the truth came home to her with a shattering clarity that threatened to tear her heart in two.

For a moment she lay still, her eyes open but seeing nothing, staring blankly into the darkness above her. Then she sat up slowly, her face white with shock and pain. Nick had rolled over on to his back and was lying very still, one arm flung up across his eyes, hiding his face from her. Erin watched him for long, silent seconds, her mind too numb to feel, while her body still throbbed with the echoes of the passion that had overwhelmed her, a throbbing that ebbed slowly, leaving a dull, nagging ache of unfulfilment. She had responded to this man as she had never responded to anyone, not even Geoff. Whatever he had asked she would have given him gladly and unthinkingly, there on the rug before the fire if that had been what he wanted.

Beside her, Nick stirred, thrusting his hand through his hair as he turned to look at her, his blue eyes dark and serious.

'God, Erin, that wasn't what I intended,' he said, his voice sounding husky and unsteady. 'I never meant that to happen, I swear it.'

Erin's eyes closed against the pain. She had known it would come but that didn't make it any easier to bear. As sanity returned she found she was trembling all over with reaction to the way she had behaved. She was no naïve schoolgirl; she had known exactly what she was doing, the risks she was taking, and yet none of that had mattered. She had never dreamed that she could want a man as much as she had wanted Nick, believing that the way she felt towards Geoff was all the desire she was capable of knowing, but those feelings were like the gentle warmth of a spring sun when compared with the searing heat of her response to this man. At least with Geoff there had been some hope of a future—with Nick there was nothing. How could there be any future with a man who had no past, a man who, if he was to be believed, did not even know his own name?

Nick was sitting up now, watching her, his uneven breathing the only sound in the otherwise silent room. The knowledge of those probing eyes on her kept Erin's head resolutely averted.

'You don't know how much I regret that,' Nick said with an effort. 'Believe me, I don't usually lose control like that. I reckon the bang on the head must have affected me more than I thought.'

Erin made a small, choking sound in her throat. She felt desperately humiliated, filled with a bitter pain so that it seemed as if she was bleeding profusely deep inside. Nick was ashamed of what had happened, he despised himself for his lack of control—but it had not been like that for her! She had wanted to give herself to this man and now he was dismissing those glorious moments of sharing, reducing them to an animal loss of control, a mental aberration, the after-effects of concussion like his loss of memory. She felt degraded and defiled, her skin crawled where Nick had touched her as if she had been tainted by some loathsome disease, and she felt physically sick.

'Erin, look at me please,' Nick said.

Unwillingly Erin lifted her eyes. She almost expected to find that Nick had changed, turned into some grotesque monster by her thoughts, but of course he had not. He looked visibly strained and ill at ease, the tautness of the muscles in his face heightening the angularity of his cheekbones, his eyes dark unfathomable pools in the firelight, but he was still Nick.

A cruel hand seemed to squeeze Erin's heart. He was Nick—but who *was* Nick? A total stranger, so alien that he might have come from another planet. He was a man about whom she knew nothing, whose existence she hadn't even dreamed of until that afternoon, and yet in those brief moments he had roused her to heights she hadn't known existed. He had made her his with the touch of his hands and his lips as surely as if he had branded her with a physical sign of his possession like some slave of long ago. She had given herself entirely into his hands to do with as he pleased and by doing so had given him a power over her that would bind her to him for ever. If she ever saw him again after tonight she would only have to look at him to remember the way he had seemed to have the power to draw her soul out of her body so that she was empty, nothing, without him.

'Forgive me,' Nick said softly, 'It won't happen again.'

He lifted his hand to brush the tangled curls away from her face and Erin flinched away from his touch as if his fingers had been fiery hot. Even now, her treacherous body reacted with a throbbing urgency to his lightest touch. Carefully she schooled her features into a mask of stony indifference.

'Don't blame yourself,' she said stiffly, her mouth forming the words automatically, 'I quite understand.'

Nick massaged the muscles at the back of his neck in the same tired gesture he had used before.

'What do you want me to say?' he asked wearily.

'Nothing.' Was that cold, hard voice really hers? 'I think it's better if we say no more about it. After all, nothing happened.'

'It damn nearly did!' Nick responded feelingly, a sudden spark lighting his eyes only to die as swiftly as it had come when he looked at her face. 'Erin, I'm sorry.'

Something seemed to snap inside Erin's mind. That was the one thing she hadn't wanted him to say! She felt such an urge of anger and pain that it almost overwhelmed her. She wanted to shout, to scream, but no words would come. When Nick moved to take her hand, her last, tenuous grip on the few remaining strands of her self-control broke and, blinded by scalding tears, she launched herself at Nick, lashing out wildly as if only physical violence could appease the pain in her heart. Her fists landed on his chest, his arm, would have struck his face if he had not jerked his head back instinctively, but still the wild fury did not ease. She struck out again and again, the harsh sobs choking her.

'I hate you!' Erin's high, angry voice seemed to splinter the air. 'Hate you! Hate you! Don't you ever touch me again, do you hear, not ever!'

But even as her fists thudded against the dark wool of his sweater she knew that it was not Nick she was lashing out against but herself. Only a short time before she had been physically afraid of Nick, had feared assault or rape—and rightly. But she had been inviting just such a reaction and, incredibly, it had been *Nick* who had called a halt. She should be grateful to him for the way he had saved her from herself—but gratitude was very far from what she was feeling.

Nick made no move to stop her or even, after that first involuntary movement, to defend himself, but waited, silent and impassive, until her fury burned itself out and she subsided, breathless and shaking, on to the rug at his side. Only then did he speak, not touching her, his quiet voice penetrating the red haze that filled her mind.

'It's all right, little one,' he said calmly, almost gently. 'I reckon I deserved that. Do you feel better now?' he added as Erin's sobs ceased. 'Got it all out of your system?'

The faintly ironic edge to his voice acted like the shock of icy water on Erin's heated brain. Her mind cleared swiftly, the hurt anger giving way to a cold calm. In that moment she became shockingly aware that her shirt was still unbuttoned down to her waist, gaping widely over the soft curves of her breasts, the pale skin gleaming golden in the firelight.

Burning with embarrassment, she fumbled clumsily with the buttons but her trembling hands would not obey her. Nick watched silently as she struggled with the recalcitrant fastenings, his sharp watchful gaze destroying any hope she had of persuading her fingers to function normally.

'Oh damn it!' Erin cried in frustration as a button broke off and spun away into the darkness.

Cool hands were laid on hers, stilling their impotent struggles. Very gently Nick eased her clenched fingers from her blouse and within seconds the buttons were fastened swiftly and easily. All the time, Nick's touch had been clinically impersonal and when he had finished he moved away from her, standing up and crossing to the window. He pushed the curtains aside and stood for a moment staring out into the black night. With half her mind Erin registered a stiffness about the way he held his head, a tension in his neck and shoulders that spoke of weariness and discomfort and the effort he was making to hide it. Then Nick let the curtain drop again and swung round to face her.

'Will you listen to me now?' he said quietly enough but with a forceful, commanding note in his voice that caught Erin's attention and held it.

Now that the blind fury had burned itself out she felt calm but exhausted. A weary lassitude filled her so that she was content simply to listen to what Nick had to say.

'None of this should have happened,' Nick said slowly. 'And I don't just mean—'

His eyes went to the disordered rug and automatically Erin's hands moved to straighten it. Her action seemed to disturb Nick and he moved restlessly, coming to sit on the edge of a chair, looking down at her soberly.

'I shouldn't be here,' he began again. 'If I hadn't had some sort of accident—I can only assume that's what happened—then I would be miles away, wherever I was going, and we would never have met. But it didn't work out like that. I did have an accident; your house was the first one I came to when I needed shelter; I'm here whether I like it or not. I can't change what's happened. I'm deeply grateful to you for all you've done for me but this whole situation is crazy and it can't go on. I'd have gone hours ago but—'

Nick left the sentence unfinished; there was no need for him to complete it, and Erin bit her lip as she remembered that he had tried to go and it had been her own foolish fear that had forced him to stay. Perhaps his innocent explanation was the true one after all. He had made no attempt to harm her, his violence earlier had been used only to teach her a lesson—a much needed one, Erin admitted ruefully.

'Well,' Nick shrugged dismissively, 'that's something else I can't change, but I can make sure I don't impose on you any longer than I have to. I can't get away tonight but if you could bring yourself to let me stay until the morning I promise you that I'll clear out first thing, just as soon as it's light. I'll get out of your life and leave you in peace.'

The room seemed strangely silent when Nick stopped speaking. The wind had died down at last and only the soft murmur of the fire registered in Erin's mind as she considered his words. She wanted him to go, wanted that peace he had spoken of, the quiet routine she had not appreciated until Nick's sudden appearance had blasted it into a thousand pieces—and yet a small, irrational part of her mind wanted him to stay. An insidious little voice whispered inside her head, telling her that without Nick life would not be peaceful—just empty.

'Erin?' Nick prompted softly.

Erin swallowed hard. Nick had been perfectly reasonable and fair; she owed him the courtesy of an equal fairness in return.

'If you think that's for the best,' she said, and was relieved to find that her voice sounded strong and calm again.

'I do. Erin, what happened between us was——'

'I don't want to talk about it, Nick!' Erin cut in sharply.

'But I do damn it!' Nick's voice rose suddenly in anger and Erin quailed inside at the sound 'I'm sorry,' he went on more quietly, 'but we can't pretend it never happened. I want you to understand.'

'What is there to understand?' Erin asked dully. She had lost control of herself, acted out of character, irrationally and stupidly, there was nothing more to say.

'Erin!' Nick sighed. 'Don't hate me for what happened—and for God's sake don't hate yourself either! We've been thrown together in totally unnatural circumstances, forced into an intimacy that happened too fast. It's a hothouse atmosphere, can't you see? Look, right now you're the only person I know in the world. You were here when I needed someone and you're a lovely girl. Maybe if we'd met some other time when I was thinking straight and we had time to get to know each other then we could have had something—but not now! It wouldn't work, you have to see that.'

Erin nodded slowly, acknowledging the sense of Nick's words, her mind admitting that he had been right to stop when he had, that he was only protecting her from herself. But her heart cried out that time or place didn't matter, what was important was how they *felt*. Then Nick spoke again and crushed those rebellious thoughts completely.

'For all I know I could be married. I may have a wife and kids somewhere, though God knows where. Until I know who I am I can't take risks with other people's feelings. I have to try and find out about myself and to do that I have to get away from here. If you can let me stay tonight I give you my word I won't even try to touch you again.'

Erin forced herself to study Nick's face, seeing the grey, shadowed look, the lines of fatigue and strain etched around his nose and mouth. She still couldn't make up her mind about him but he was hurt and tired, it was almost midnight on a bitterly cold night and she had first-hand experience of the appalling conditions outside. She couldn't throw him out now.

'You can have the spare bed,' she said, knowing there was no other answer she could give.

CHAPTER FIVE

THE room was strangely gloomy when Erin opened her eyes and lay drowsily, wondering what had woken her. Her mind was still fogged with sleep and although she knew, with a half-formed sense of foreboding, that there was something she should remember she could not quite define what it was. Then the knock at the door was repeated and Nick's voice spoke her name and she remembered, images flooding back with a vividness that made her groan and wish she was still asleep. Thoughts of Nick had kept her awake half the night, he had haunted her dreams, and she wasn't ready to face him yet.

But the door was already opening and Nick came into the room carrying a steaming mug of coffee. Finding herself jolted suddenly wide awake, Erin eyed him uneasily, trying to judge his mood as he placed the mug on the bedside table. She felt very small and vulnerable lying down while Nick loomed over her, his dark head almost reaching the heavy oak beams on the ceiling.

He looked slightly better this morning, the blue eyes less shadowed by the strain that had showed in them the night before. He looked vitally alive and—Erin's breath seemed to catch in her throat—devastatingly attractive. Seeing him in the daylight for the first time, she was suddenly intensely aware of the small details she had missed before, the glossy sheen on the dark brown hair, the way those startlingly blue eyes were ringed with a circle of darker blue at the edge of the iris, the intriguing contrast between the harsh power of his facial bone structure and the warm, rather sensual mouth. All of which added up to a man one could never pass by in a crowd; a man too sensually disturbing for any woman to be comfortable with the fact that she was alone with him in her bedroom.

'Do you always sleep this late?' Nick enquired, installing himself comfortably at the bottom of the bed and leaning back against the wall.

'I suppose you've been up for hours!' Erin commented, the memory of the thoughts that had kept her awake making her voice tart. Nick inclined his head in agreement.

'I couldn't sleep,' he said briefly. 'Are you going to drink that coffee or not?'

'I'll drink it when I'm ready!' Erin snapped, painfully aware of the fact that, althought her nightdress was a long-sleeved Victorian style, it was still a nightdress and she was reluctant to expose herself to Nick's probing gaze in it. She could not forget that he knew exactly what she looked like under the soft blue cotton and that memory was not one she cared to consider too closely.

'Suit yourself—but don't blame me if it goes cold.'

'Are you always so cheerful in the mornings?' Erin demanded, uneasiness making her ill-tempered.

Nick considered for a moment then shot her a look filled with wry amusement.

'I'll have to pass on that one,' he stated drily. 'We'll consider it again tomorrow or the day after.'

'We will not!' Erin declared forcefully, sitting up swiftly, her earlier reservations completely forgotten. 'You won't be here tomorrow! We had an agreement remember—you stayed one night, that's all. You're leaving today.'

'That was the arrangement,' Nick agreed but something about his tone jarred on Erin's ears and she glanced at his face suspiciously.

The blue eyes met her scrutiny quite candidly but their guileless expression did nothing to reassure Erin;

in fact it had quite the opposite effect, arousing new and disturbing doubts in her mind. Just what was Nick playing at? For he was up to something, she was sure of that. Erin was forced to wonder whether she had been hopelessly deceived. Perhaps he had never really planned to go in the first place, perhaps he had some very good reason for wanting to leave. All her earlier fears and suspicions came back with a vengeance.

'Just what——' she began angrily, but Nick broke in on her.

'Calm down, little lady,' he said evenly. 'There's nothing to get in a panic about. I have some good news and some bad news, which do you want first?'

Erin sighed her exasperation. He was being deliberately provoking! She had to struggle to keep her temper from flaring up.

'The good news I suppose,' she said ungraciously, stretching out a hand for the mug of coffee. She had a feeling she was going to need it. Her heart was beating in an uncomfortably jerky way and she had to put the mug down in her lap so as not to betray the sudden unsteadiness of her hands.

'So what is the good news?' she demanded a moment later when Nick did not seem prepared to enlighten her.

'Two things really. One, the power's back on—see——'

He moved to press the switch on the bedside lamp to demonstrate and Erin blinked at the sudden brightness.

'And, two, I've found the bag.'

'The bag?' Erin echoed, puzzled. Then she remembered and sat up swiftly, coming dangerously close to spilling her coffee. 'Your bag? But Nick, that's marvellous!'

Erin's voice revealed a genuine pleasure in what he had told her. As she had lain awake she had tried to imagine how it must feel to be unable to remember anything about yourself, even your name, and had found the experience distinctly unnerving even though it was only imaginary. Her thoughts had given her new insights into Nick's state of mind and now that he was nearer to learning the truth she was unreservedly happy for him.

'Where was it?'

'Just outside the door—almost buried in the snow. I must have dropped it there. I'm surprised you didn't see it.'

'It was probably pretty well covered even then,' Erin said thoughtfully, remembering how her attention had been on the inside of the house; she hadn't thought to look elsewhere.

Nick nodded vaguely, his thoughts seeming to be on other things. He was staring down at his hands, twisting the gold signet ring on his finger in the restless, preoccupied gesture Erin had seen him use before.

'Well don't keep me in suspense!' she exclaimed impatiently. 'What did you find?'

Nick's eyes swung up to her face, very blue against the dark tan of his skin and totally expressionless. Whatever he was feeling he was keeping it well hidden.

'Very little,' he said slowly. 'Some clothes, shaving things, a couple of books—oh, and a bottle of brandy.'

'Brandy?' Erin could not believe she had heard right.

Nick inclined his head slightly in agreement.

'Maybe I planned to get roaring drunk,' he said, his tone light, almost indifferent, but Erin sensed a disturbing tension about him and the wary, guarded expression marked his face once more giving her the distinct impression he was holding something back.

'And that was all?' she prompted.

'Yes.' The single syllable came curtly, defensively.

'But it can't be!' Disappointment sharpened Erin's voice. She had been so sure that when they found the missing bag it would contain something that would give Nick's memory the jolt it needed. A few clothes and books told them nothing other than the fact that he had been travelling light—but from where, to where? 'There must have been something else.'

'What for instance? A birth certificate? Family tree? Diaries to cover the last thirty-three years?' Nick's biting sarcasm stung Erin painfully.

'Don't be ridiculous!' she said reproachfully. 'You know what I mean—a driving licence or a cheque book—credit cards—something with your name on it.'

'No,' Nick said stonily.

Was it really just for Nick's sake that she was so disappointed? Hadn't she hoped for something that would have proved him to be just the innocent victim of an accident, something to ease her conscience and her outraged common sense over her behaviour last night? But they were as far away from the truth as ever. Nick was still the dark enigma of the previous night, a man with no name, a man of shadows and mystery, a man she could not trust.

'I'm sorry,' she said and meant it—for both of them.

Nick's eyes slid away from her and he frowned down at the patchwork bedspread.

'Did you make this?' he asked unexpectedly, but as Erin gave an automatic response she was sure that he was not really interested in her answer but was concerned with other, more personal thoughts.

'Clever girl,' he murmured, one long finger idly tracing the hexagonal shapes of the pattern. 'You're not at all what I expected,' he added abruptly, lifting his eyes to hers once more, the clear blue gaze unnervingly direct.

Erin found his sudden intense scrutiny perturbing and her hands clenched tightly around her mug.

'How do you know what you expected?' she challenged sharply.

Nick's frown darkened and his hand stilled suddenly. '*Touché*,' he muttered with grim irony. 'I can still *think* you know! All right,' he went on, controlling his voice with evident effort, 'put yourself in my place. If you woke up in a bedroom filled with almost antique furniture, with embroidered samplers dated 1898 or thereabouts on the walls, would you expect to find a young girl wearing denim jeans and what looked like an expensive designer sweater living here alone?'

'I designed the sweater myself—it's my job—and the furniture came with the house when I inherited it from my great aunt.'

Erin's voice was hesitant on the last words. Was it safe to tell him so much about herself?

'Why you?'

It seemed just a polite enquiry but Erin could not bring herself to answer it. Nick's hand clenched on the bedspread.

'OK,' he said gruffly. 'I've no right to ask. Forget it.'

'No, it's all right.' There was no harm in telling him this, surely? 'Great Aunt Bee never married and I was her only great niece. We were very close and she knew how much I loved this cottage. No one else visited her much but I loved coming here. As a child I used to——'

Erin broke off, Nick's expression silencing her. It had been fleeting, nothing more than a flicker across his face, but it was enough to make her study him more closely, seeing too late the tension in his neck and shoulders, the emptiness in his eyes. She had been chattering on about her past and hadn't stopped to think how Nick might feel. Frantically she hunted for a way of changing the subject.

'Was that the bad news—about there being nothing helpful in the bag, I mean?'

'No, that was just disappointing.'

Nick spoke nonchalantly but this time Erin was alert to every nuance of his tone and she saw through the assumed casualness, recognising the careful cover-up for what it was.

'The bad news is something else—we're snowed in,' Nick told her bluntly.

'But we can't be!' Erin exclaimed, her voice filled with frank disbelief. Nick dismissed her words with an impatient gesture.

'It's been snowing all night and it's still coming down. Take a look for yourself if you don't believe me,' he said, sliding off the bed and crossing to the window.

When he jerked the curtains apart Erin stared in shock and horror at the transformation of the familiar landscape into a hostile, frozen wilderness by what seemed like a solid wall of snow. Still more was falling from an ominously heavy sky. Now she understood the strange, greyish light in the room when she had first woken up.

'Get the picture? I can see you do. The problem is,' Nick went on, lounging back against the wall and pushing his hands deep into his pockets, 'what are we—or, rather, you—going to do about it?'

'I can't do anything!' Erin said, startled. 'It's snowing—I can't stop it!'

'Don't be deliberately obtuse!' Nick snapped. 'You know very well what I mean.'

He lifted a hand to brush angrily at a lock of dark hair that had fallen forward over his forehead, drawing her eyes to the ugly bruise that showed shockingly clearly even in the uncertain light of a winter morning. Erin drew in her breath sharply. She had forgotten just how nasty it was and the sight of it made her wonder just how much effort Nick was making to ignore his injury. Dragging her mind away from that uncomfortable thought, she tried to concentrate on what Nick was saying.

'Erin, try and understand.' Nick spoke slowly and distinctly as if explaining something to a difficult child. 'The snow has been piling up all night, there are drifts God knows how deep outside and the roads must be completely blocked. No one can get to us and we—I—can't get out.'

Slowly, it dawned on Erin just what he was trying to say and her eyes widened in shock and consternation.

'You mean you're not leaving today?'

'Not unless you happen to have a sledge and a team of huskies hidden away somewhere. It looks like you're stuck with me.'

'But you can't stay!' Erin cried. 'I don't want you to! I mean—can't you clear a path?' she finished lamely.

Nick's mouth twisted bitterly at her reaction.

'Sorry to disappoint you,' he said coldly, 'but I doubt if a snow plough could get through that lot.'

Abruptly he swung away to stare out of the window, his expression as cold and bleak as the landscape outside.

'Erin, I realise you can't wait to see the back of me,' he said in a voice that was tight with suppressed anger, 'and, believe me, I'd get out now if I could—I don't want to stay any more than you want me to—but it can't be done!'

Erin sighed faintly. It was partly because she did *not* want to see the back of him that he had to go. Quite aside from the too obvious dangers in having an unknown quantity like Nick in her house like this, there was another, potentially more devastating risk that she ran if he stayed. Last night had shown her that she was dangerously attracted to Nick and the longer he remained in the house the more chance there was that she might behave like that again, letting her feelings take control against all rational reasoning. She felt sick with panic at the thought. How could she have felt such passion for a man she knew nothing about, could never know anything about if his loss of memory was permanent?

And if it's even real, added the cold voice of reason in the back of her mind, making her stomach clench painfully on a physical pang of fear. She had only Nick's word for the fact that he had lost his memory at all!

'If we are trapped as you say, we could be stuck here for days,' she said slowly, choosing her words with infinite care, watching Nick closely for his reaction. 'And that would cause all sorts of problems for you.'

Slowly Nick turned to face her, his eyes narrowing speculatively.

'What sort of problems?' he asked softly.

Erin's hands closed on the sheet that covered her, folding it over and over nervously. She didn't like the way Nick was looking at her and there had been a distinctly hard edge to the quietly spoken words. There was a queasy sensation in the pit of her stomach at the thought that he realised only too well that she was testing him.

'Well, there must be someone who'll wonder where you are—someone who'll worry,' she persevered.

'Very possibly,' Nick said flatly and something about the way he spoke revived Erin's earlier suspicion that he was keeping something from her.

'There was something else in that bag, wasn't there? Something you're not telling me. Nick, what is it? I want to know!'

For a moment she thought he was going to refuse to answer. Heavy eyelids hooded the blue eyes and the muscles in his jaw tightened ominously. Then, appearing to reconsider, he pulled something from the back pocket of his jeans and tossed it towards her. The paper fluttered in the air for a moment then drifted slowly down to land on the bedspread close to Erin's hand. Nick watched impassively as she picked it up.

As soon as she saw the photograph Erin realised with a painful lurch of her heart just why Nick had tried to conceal it from her. It was worn and creased as if from much handling and the fair-haired young woman could have been anyone, a sister, girlfriend, cousin, but the sturdy child in her arms was quite a different matter. The little boy had a shock of dark brown hair and a pair of wide blue eyes fringed with long, thick lashes, and although his face still had the soft roundness of a baby just developing into a toddler it took very little effort to see that in a year or two he would be a small mirror image of Nick himself.

He's married, married, married; the words pounded in Erin's head like a physical ache as her eyes went back to the smiling face of the woman holding the child and she almost cried out at the wave of desolation that swept through her. There was no reason for her to feel this way, none at all, she told herself angrily, but she couldn't drive the feeling from her mind as she turned the photograph over. There was nothing written on the back, nothing to help Nick—or herself—there.

'That was inside one of the books.' Nick's voice broke in on her thoughts, startling her so that her eyes went swiftly to the dark figure by the window.

'Is she your wife?'

'What do you think?' Nick parried the question belligerently, turning it back on her.

'She's very lovely,' Erin tried again. 'And the little boy's gorgeous. What's his name?'

The question wasn't part of the test. In the moment she had seen the photograph Erin had forgotten all about her doubts as to the truth of Nick's story and it had slipped out before she realised quite what she had said. She bit her lip hard, cursing her foolishness when she saw the sudden flash of violence in Nick's eyes.

'How the hell should I know?' he demanded savagely. 'I don't know who he is, where he is, what he is—Godammit, I don't know!'

Nick's words fell on Erin like physical blows as she shrank back on the pillows, terrified by the sudden explosive fury she had triggered off with her thoughtless words.

'I'm—I'm sorry,' she stammered. 'I didn't think.'

'You didn't think!' Nick's response was a bitter parody of Erin's words. He pressed his hands hard against his temples as if they ached unbearably. 'You didn't think,' he went on more quietly, but with a raw note in his voice that twisted something sharply in Erin's heart. 'You don't think and I can't stop! I've gone over and over it till I think I'll go mad and still I can't remember!'

Without warning Nick slumped down on the bed, his eyes closed.

'I was lying under a tree,' he said slowly and painfully, his whole body taut with the effort he was making to remember. 'I can remember the tree—it had been split in two at some time, probably by lightning—and I know everything that happened after that, but before then——' Nick's hands clenched as if he was trying to grasp something before it slipped away from him. 'Before then it's blank, empty—nothing!'

'Nick, don't!'

Completely forgetting all her earlier fears, Erin flung back the covers and swung her legs on to the floor, hurrying to Nick's side, wanting only to help him.

'Please don't!' she begged, taking hold of his hand and gripping it tightly. 'Don't torture yourself like this!'

'That woman,' Nick said slowly and his voice was dead, no expression in the dull tones, 'I don't know her or the child—I don't recognise them, they don't touch anything in me. Surely if she's my wife—if he's my son—I should feel *something*!'

It was as if the world had suddenly stood still. Erin could not believe the joy she felt at Nick's words. All colour drained from her cheeks as she realised just what she had been thinking. She had been *glad* that Nick did not remember his wife and son, but especially his wife.

Was she really so unprincipled that she could feel happiness at someone else's expense?

Nick turned to her then and she shivered involuntarily when she saw the raw emotion in his eyes. He couldn't be acting, he just couldn't!

'It will come,' she said gently, longing to lift a hand to smooth away the lines of strain scored into his skin. 'Give it time, Nick. You'll remember, I know you will.'

'I wish I had your confidence.'

Nick's voice held the tiniest hint of his earlier dry humour. He seemed to recover very quickly from the black desolation that had gripped him—or did he? There had been other times when he had suddenly switched to that wry flippancy—she would watch more closely, observe his reactions more carefully next time.

'They're not real,' Nick was saying, returning to the subject of the photograph. 'They're just images. *You're* real and, right now, you mean more to me than they do.'

The sudden, exultant soaring of her heart made Erin's head swim but almost immediately her joy was destroyed by a savage sense of guilt. Now she recognised the feeling she had experienced when she had seen the woman in the photograph. It was jealousy—a hurting, irrational jealousy of an unknown woman simply because she was Nick's wife. Dazedly Erin studied Nick's face, trying to read in it just what it was about this man that made her think and act in a way that was totally alien to the person she believed herself to be, and as she did so Geoff's words crept into her mind.

'I never meant it to happen,' he had said, 'but when I met Becky I knew I couldn't live without her. Without her I can't function, the world seems empty.'

But Geoff had been talking about love. What she felt for Nick wasn't love, it was desire pure and simple—though there was nothing pure about the feelings he aroused in her, Erin amended wryly. From the first, even as he lay asleep, she had registered an aura of sensual excitement about him, sensing it in the air as an animal scents an intruder into its territory. Then, last night, Nick's kisses had awoken a raw, uncontrolled streak in her nature that she had never known she possessed—but passion was all it was.

Nick moved restlessly, getting to his feet to stare broodingly out at the snow, and, freed from the intoxicating power of his closeness, Erin's chaotic thoughts calmed and slowed, turning to an even more uncomfortable train of thought. She had always believed that love had to grow slowly and steadily as it had, for her, with Geoff. But the break-up of that relationship had taught her that it wasn't always like that. Love could come out of the blue, fully formed and devastating, tearing your world apart with the shock of realisation. Knowing she felt *something* for Nick, admitting to an intensity of attraction towards him that made her feelings for Geoff insipid by comparison, and faced with the prospect of being trapped with him in this dangerous intimacy, Erin shivered in icy panic at the thought of the consequences for herself if she should ever come to feel more than she did now.

Erin stared out of the living room window, unable to drag her eyes away from the devastation wrought by the heavy blanket of white that stretched across the countryside, obliterating every landmark. If she had been on her own she might actually have enjoyed the idea of her enforced hibernation, but Nick's presence altered the situation completely. The thought so unsettled her that she snapped forcefully at Nick when he suggested checking their food supplies.

'Don't you think you're over-reacting? The snow could be gone by tomorrow.'

'No chance. The only thing that will clear this lot is a

downpour, so I suggest you start praying for rain. If it's
any consolation, I don't like being stuck here either—I
do have one or two more important things I could be
doing. Now, are you coming?'

The ominous hardening of Nick's voice had Erin out
of her chair before she had time to think.

'Coming sergeant-major, sir!' she said with a flash of
satire, saluting smartly as she spoke. Then, as a thought
struck her, she glanced at Nick curiously. 'You're not in
the army, are you?'

Nick's response was a decisively negative shake of his
head. 'Definitely not,' he said curtly.

How could he be so sure? Erin felt as if the ground
had rocked beneath her feet. She had believed in him.
Had her trust been too easily given?

'You can't know that!' she said sharply. 'Not unless
you've remembered something!'

'I'd tell you if I had.' Nick's tone, the coldness of his
eyes, warned her to let things be but Erin defied that
warning.

'Then how——' she began belligerently, but Nick did
not let her finish.

'Damn it, Erin, I can't answer my own questions,
never mind yours! I just *know*—leave it at that!'

'Well, if not the army, what about the navy?' Erin
persisted, pursuing her question doggedly as she
followed him out to the kitchen. 'Or the air force?'

Her questioning met with no response as Nick
opened cupboards and assessed their contents swiftly
and efficiently—as efficiently as he had dealt with the
normally troublesome coal fire earlier, Erin remembered—which was evidence of a capable, practical
sort of mind. What part of his buried past had taught
him that? If that past was indeed buried, she caught
herself up hastily.

Her thoughts went to the bag Nick had found. He
had been quite open about letting her see its contents,

in fact he had left it in the living room when he had
gone to make fresh coffee, giving Erin the perfect
opportunity to check it for herself—an opportunity she
had had no compunction in taking. His actions were
those of a man with nothing to hide.

Not that the bag had told her anything. Her search of
it had revealed only a grey Shetland wool sweater and
black jeans that could be worn by anyone in their lei-
sure time and a couple of detective novels that were as
anonymous as everything else about him, the sort of
thing one picked up at a railway station or an airport to
while away a long journey. She couldn't see Nick
behind a desk or in any mundane nine-to-five job and
those hands were clearly not used to heavy manual
work—which left what?

The mention of the army had produced a surprisingly
forceful reaction but now, trying to imagine Nick in
uniform and failing, Erin felt that the idea of the forces
was way off the mark. The elemental, untamed quality
in him seemed too strong to be confined in any such
way. There was too much of the loner, the individual
about him.

'Or there's always the police—plainclothes—C.I.D.—
Do you think you're a detective?'

'Erin, I don't know!' Nick exploded in the same
second that the frightening realisation that she still had
no evidence that he was even on the right side of the
law closed Erin's throat over any further questions.

'The food situation's better than I expected,' Nick
went on more quietly after an uncomfortable pause
during which Erin's thoughts headed off down a very
unpleasant path indeed. 'That's an unexpected bonus,'
he added, indicating the brand new fridge-freezer that
had been a housewarming present from Erin's father.
'Somehow I got the impression you weren't the sort of
girl who bothered with such modern luxuries—you
don't have a television for one thing.'

'Oh that!' Erin laughed. She had never been addicted to 'the box', preferring her collection of cassettes because she could knit or sew while listening to them. 'I don't have time to . . .'

Her voice trailed off when she saw Nick's face. He was staring at her but seemed to be looking straight through her as if she did not exist. His sudden abstraction worried and frightened her.

'Nick!' she cried sharply and saw the sudden jolt as he dragged his attention back to her.

'Coal,' he said inconsequentially, his voice dull and automatic. 'Have we got enough?'

'I—I think so,' Erin stammered, still trying to adjust to his momentary preoccupation. It was as if he had gone away from her into some other world where she couldn't reach him. 'The fuel store's here.'

She opened a door off the kitchen but Nick spared the heaped coal only the most cursory of glances. His movements seemed slow and disjointed like those of a clockwork toy that has almost run down. Abruptly he reached for his cigarettes with a hand that shook noticeably. Erin watched him anxiously, noting once more how the bruise on his head had spread and darkened overnight so that it lay like an ugly stain above his eye.

'Nick, are you all right?'

He didn't answer and she saw that he had abandoned his attempt to light the cigarette and was once more twisting the signet ring round and round in the gesture she had come to recognise as expressive of his disturbed thoughts. There had been other small gestures, hesitations, fleeting expressions throughout the morning, small and insignificant in themselves, but taken altogether—

'You should be more careful!' Erin exclaimed, fear, worry and guilt at her own forgetfulness combining to make her voice shrill. 'You ought to be resting!'

'Erin, don't fuss!' Nick snarled, the blue eyes blazing into hers.

Erin swallowed hard. If he was concussed he should be kept quiet; arguing with him was the worst thing she could do. But it wasn't easy to show concern for a man who stubbornly tried to hide any sign of weakness and it was made all the harder by the fact that she could never give her sympathy whole-heartedly. But the pallor of Nick's face was real enough; he could hardly fake that.

'I'll make you a drink,' she said, making a determined effort to stay calm. 'You look as if you could do with one.'

Nick sat at the table watching her silently as she prepared a pot of tea, one hand toying restlessly with his lighter. The nervous movement stilled suddenly as, remembering that sweet tea was supposed to be good for shock, Erin thoughtlessly spooned sugar into the cup and stirred it thoroughly. Nick's fingers tightened on the lighter as if he would snap it in two.

'My brain may be scrambled,' he said, with biting coldness, 'but I have not been reduced to the level of a complete idiot! *If* I took sugar in my tea I am still capable of putting it in myself.'

For a second a flush of angry colour showed along the high cheekbones then faded as swiftly as it had come leaving Nick's face white and empty. Slamming his fist down on the table he swore violently, but the despondent slump of his shoulders told Erin that his fury was directed at himself, not at her. She had an almost overwhelming desire to take him in her arms and hold him. If only he would open up, talk to her instead of keeping everything inside! But already the shuttered mask was coming down over his face, the invisible, intangible barriers he built up around himself were back in place.

'I'm sorry,' Nick said flatly, his blue eyes darkly

shadowed. 'I didn't mean that. I'm afraid I don't find myself very easy to live with at the moment.'

The grim understatement caught Erin on the raw and she flinched inside at the thought of all that the words might hide.

'Wouldn't it help to talk about it?'

'There's nothing to talk about, can't you see that? There's nothing *there*, just a great black, bottomless pit where my past should be! I feel as if I don't exist.'

Nick's voice was filled with such an intensity of impotent anger that it hurt Erin physically to hear it. Suddenly he lifted his hands in a brusque, dismissive gesture.

'But that's my problem, not yours.'

That hurt. There was no reason why it should but it hurt all the same.

'But I want to help!'

'Erin, it's my problem!' Nick said harshly. 'It's my head, my memory, and——'

He clamped his mouth shut on what he had been about to say and got to his feet, reaching for the mug of tea.

'I'll take this upstairs,' he said, his tone once more ruthlessly controlled. 'I'll come back when I'm fit for human company.'

CHAPTER SIX

ERIN sliced the peel from the potatoes with unnecessary savagery, her brusque movements mirroring her troubled thoughts as she listened for some sound from the bedroom above. Nick's restless pacing had stopped an hour or more ago and since then there had been total silence from his room. She couldn't help wondering what he had found to think about in all that time when he had nothing to remember.

She switched on the radio as a defence against the oppressive silence, thinking ruefully just how much had happened since she had done exactly the same thing the night before—and yet, deep down, nothing had really changed either.

The chips were just turning an attractive golden brown when Nick appeared in the doorway as suddenly and silently as he had on the day before. One swift glance at his face warned Erin to keep the atmosphere light so she forced herself to smile a welcome.

'I'll bet you're ready for this,' she said, keeping her attention carefully on her cooking.

As Nick murmured something that might have been agreement, the time signal for the news sounded on the radio and Erin turned, a plate in either hand, just in time to see him stretch out a hand and switch it off with a swift, impatient movement.

'Hey!' she said reproachfully into the sudden silence. 'I was listening to that!'

'I wasn't,' was the unconcerned response.

'Now look!' Erin banged the plates down on the table, her temper threatening to get the better of her determination to keep things light. 'I may have to put

up with you being here because I have no alternative,
but that doesn't give you the right to take over! I
wanted to listen to the news.'

'And I don't.'

Nick's tone made Erin take an instinctive step
backwards, afraid of what his next move might be. She
could read nothing of his mood from his face but there
was something about the way he stood, a stubborn set
to his jaw that told her she would be unwise to push the
point any further. Unnervingly she was reminded of the
moment Nick had first appeared in the kitchen the day
before and her stomach contracted with a cold sense of
fear. He had switched off the radio then, too, silencing
another news bulletin. A chilling sensation spread
through Erin's veins. What was it he didn't want her to
hear?

When Nick moved she flinched instinctively but he had
only pulled out a chair from the table, lowering himself
into it, his attention apparently on the food in front of him.

'It would only depress you,' he said, his conversa-
tional tone very much at odds with the controlled
aggression Erin had seen in him only seconds before,
though the tautness of the muscles in the broad
shoulders was a clear indication that she would be most
unwise to believe he had fully relaxed again.

His last comment was true enough. The news, with its
reports of death and destruction in various parts of the
world, might well depress her, but how could Nick
know what sort of items there might be unless—oh
God!—he *had* been lying to her all along.

'Your meal's getting cold,' Nick remarked and his
carefully tolerant tone sparked an explosion of anger in
Erin's mind, blasting away the paralysing terror.

'Who the hell do you think you are!' she stormed,
blind to the perceptible tightening of Nick's mouth.
'Walking in here uninvited and unwanted and telling me
what I can and can't do! This is *my* house!'

She knew she was risking trouble but she was beyond caring as she gave vent to the emotions that had been stored up inside her all day, flinging words at Nick without a thought for the consequences.

'If you're going to stay here which, unfortunately for me, seems unavoidable, then it's time we came to some arrangement—like understanding that you're here on sufferance and *I'll* decide what happens. So when I say I want the radio on we'll have it on!'

Oh, this was crazy! Nine days out of ten she never even switched the radio on, let alone listened to the news, and now here she was fighting for just that as if it was the most important thing in the world to her—which it might be, a coldly fearful voice inside her head added, but her mind flinched away from considering the full implications of that thought.

Nick's eyebrows had lifted slightly at Erin's outburst but he made no other response, though the blue eyes never left her face for a second. Foolishly, Erin took his silence for acquiescence though she admitted to frank amazement at the ease with which he had conceded the victory.

'I think you've got the message,' she said rather breathlessly and turned to switch on the radio once again.

Nick's chair made an ugly scraping sound on the floor as he stood up swiftly. The radio was snatched away, lifted high above Erin's head. Then, perfectly calmly, his face still set in that hard, inimical mask that made it appear to have been carved from stone, Nick removed the plug from the socket in the wall, pulling the flex away from the radio and dropping it on to the table beside his plate. A moment later the batteries landed on top of it.

'Give those back!'

Without thinking Erin lunged towards Nick, her hand going out to take the batteries from him. He had

clearly anticipated her reaction however and, banging
the radio down on the worktop with total disregard for
its safety, he flung out a hand to repulse her attack,
brushing her aside with an insulting lack of effort.

'None of that, lady!' he warned roughly, catching
hold of Erin's wrists, gripping them tightly and holding
her at arms' length, a cold anger burning deep in those
electric blue eyes. 'I said, none of that!'

The low voice was definitely dangerous now, the
suppressed anger all the more frightening because Nick
had never once raised his voice above conversationål
level. With a sickening sense of defeat Erin acknowledged that her efforts were getting her nowhere. Nick
was holding her easily, apparently without effort. If she
was to struggle any more he would simply tighten his
grip, exert a little more pressure ånd she would be
helpless.

Stop now! she told herself. Don't risk antagonising
him any more. For the moment at least discretion
seemed the wisest policy. Nick waited calmly until she
stood mutinously silent at his side before he released
her wrists abruptly.

'Now perhaps I can have my meal in peace,' he said
curtly.

The uneasy silence that descended persisted throughout the meal, broken only at the very end by Nick's
offer to make the coffee. As he crossed to the stove Erin
eyed the small pile of batteries still lying on the table.
She could easily snatch them while Nick's back was
turned—but that would mean risking another attack.

Erin shivered. She had needed that warning, needed a
reminder of just how foolish she would be to trust this
man unquestioningly. In her concern for the sudden
weakness he had shown that morning she had come
close to forgetting that her own safety should be her
first consideration. Nick's reaction had been excessive
to say the least.

'What's so dreadful about listening to the news?' she challenged suddenly, feeling slightly more confident when she did not have to look at Nick's face. 'What are you trying to hide?'

'Oh, so that's it!' The laugh that accompanied Nick's words was harshly cynical, totally without humour. 'You think I'm afraid I'll hear something about myself do you? What a vivid imagination you have to be sure. Personally, I very much doubt that anything I've done is headline material so drop it like a good girl.'

'I *won't* drop it!' It couldn't be just her imagination. There had to be more to it than that, some particular item he hadn't wanted her to hear, whether consciously or subconsciously. 'You're the one who started World War Three over this without any sort of explanation!'

'Give me patience!' Nick sighed. 'Since when did I have to explain everything to you?—No, don't answer that, I can guess. Since I walked into your house uninvited, right? OK, try this then—I don't know. It was as much a surprise to me as it was to you.'

Nick's mouth twisted bitterly at the mistrusting expression on Erin's face.

'You asked,' he murmured with cynical flippancy.

'I asked because I've every right to know.'

The kettle was slammed down on the worktop and Erin swallowed hard. If only she had put the radio on sooner, while Nick was still upstairs. She might have caught an earlier news bulletin and heard something that would at least give her a clue as to whether she should hate this man or help him—or would that be more terrifying than not knowing? Shut in with him like this, perhaps ignorance was bliss.

'OK, you do have every right to know.' Nick had come back to the table, handing Erin a mug of coffee before he sat down opposite her. 'But I can't tell you what I don't know myself. If I wanted to prove *who* I am it would be so much easier, but how do I prove nothing? Thinking about it doesn't help—it's like banging your head against a brick wall except that it still hurts when you stop.

Automatically Erin noticed the sudden jump to wry humour that had happened so many times before. A dawning suspicion about that and the way the darkness of Nick's eyes belied his flippant tone coloured his next words in a new and very different way.

'Sometimes, just for a moment, I've felt as if there was something there, as if all I had to do was reach out and grasp it. But when I try to pin it down it disintegrates and there's nothing, just an ache. Thirty-three years gone like that!' Nick snapped his fingers to emphasise his words.

Erin drew a slow, uneven breath, wondering if she dared speak the thought that was in her mind.

'Perhaps you should *make* yourself listen to the news,' she said tentatively, testing the ground carefully.

Nick's head came up swiftly. 'Why?' he demanded.

'Well, for one thing, a local broadcast might tell you if a car had been found—we still don't know for sure that no one else was hurt.'

A sharp, painful sensation stabbed at Erin as she saw the sudden flash of Nick's eyes. Had she touched on some private nightmare? It was a struggle to make herself go on.

'And for another, just listening to it might trigger off something, jolt you into remembering.'

'Erin, I can't!' The iron control had slipped momentarily but a second later it had snapped back into place. The blue eyes held Erin's, a bitter humour clouding them. 'After all, we don't know what we might find out and when we're stuck here alone like this it might be better for your peace of mind if we didn't probe too deeply. From what I understand of it, amnesia can mean there's something you can't bear to remember and God knows what that could be!'

'It can't be anything so very dreadful!'

Erin was stunned at what she had said, shocked by the conviction in her voice. Until she had heard the words spoken aloud she had no idea they had even formed inside her head. Nick's smile in response was tinged with a bitter irony.

'You sound so very sure,' he murmured sardonically. 'Erin, my sweet innocent, how the hell can you know?'

Erin shook her head confusedly. She didn't *know*! She had spoken from her heart without any rational evidence on which to base her assumption. She started nervously as Nick leaned forward suddenly, his eyes probing deep into hers.

'You can't trust me,' he said with soft intensity. 'I don't know what makes me act as I do. I do things without understanding why and it could mean everything or nothing, I have no way of knowing, but for your own sake you should keep your distance, mistrust everything I do.'

You can't trust me—the words rang in Erin's head. Surely only a man who *could* be trusted would warn her against himself in this way? From the start, Nick had shown a sensitive appreciation of her position. He had understood the dangers of it far better than she had herself which was why he had broken away from her last night, something Erin had been incapable of doing for herself. Something twisted sharply in Erin's heart at the thought that Nick's lovemaking might be one of those actions that ultimately meant nothing.

'So last night . . .'

'Last night?' Nick sighed deeply. 'Last night was different. Erin, you have to understand, right now I know no one but you and you're a very lovely girl. I could fall for you in a big way if I let myself.'

There it was again, that crazy, inexplicable leap of her heart at Nick's words. Why should it mean so very much simply to know that he found her attractive? Erin struggled for composure but her efforts were in vain when Nick spoke again.

'I don't want to hurt you but you have to know the truth for your own sake. You must understand that it can't happen, not between the two of us. We have no future you and I—I can't drag you in with me. If you knew how much I despise myself for what happened last night—I was confused, half out of my mind, and you were there. It wasn't *you*, it could have been any woman, I didn't care.'

There was a bitter taste in Erin's mouth, a queasy, sick sensation in the pit of her stomach. He had *used* her simply because she was there and so foolishly, crazily willing. Her mind reeled as if from the force of a physical blow. Like a child fascinated by the flames she had ventured too near the fire and been savagely burned, but she had learned her lesson, she would never go near the fire again.

All this time Nick had held himself well away from her but when he placed his hand over hers where they lay on the table top the light touch seemed to rip through her viciously, tearing her to pieces. Violently she shook it off, springing to her feet with a movement that sent her chair crashing to the floor.

'Don't touch me!'

The high-pitched cry echoed round the small room and Erin shuddered to think that the sound was her own voice.

'What sort of a creature are you? You're not a man, you're an animal! Any woman would do!' The words almost choked her but she forced them out. 'But it wasn't just any woman—it was me—and I won't be used like that! I'm not just some cheap whore, bought and paid for so you can appease your desires without compunction, I'm a person, I have feelings, and you walked all over them! Well let me tell you, Mr Whoever-you-are, you lay one finger on

Win "Instantly" right now in another way

...try our Preview Service

Get 4 FREE full-length Harlequin Romance books

Plus this elegant jewelry bag

Plus a surprise free gift

Plus lots more!

Our love stories are popular everywhere...and WE'RE CELE-BRATING with free birthday prizes—free gifts—and a fabulous no-strings offer.

Simply try our Preview Service. With your trial, you get SNEAK PREVIEW RIGHTS to six new HARLEQUIN ROMANCE novels a month—months before they are in stores—with 10%-OFF retail on any books you keep (just $1.75 each)—and Free Home Delivery besides.

THERE IS NO CATCH. You're not required to buy a single book, ever. You may even cancel Preview Service privileges anytime, if you want. The free gifts are yours anyway, as tokens of our appreciation.

It's a super sweet deal if ever there was one. Try us and see.

LAST CHANCE EXTRA! Sign up for Preview

Service now, get lots of free gifts *AND* automatically qualify to WIN THIS AND *ALL* 1986 "Super Celebration" PRIZES & PRIZE FEATURES. It's a fabulous bonanza—*don't miss it!*

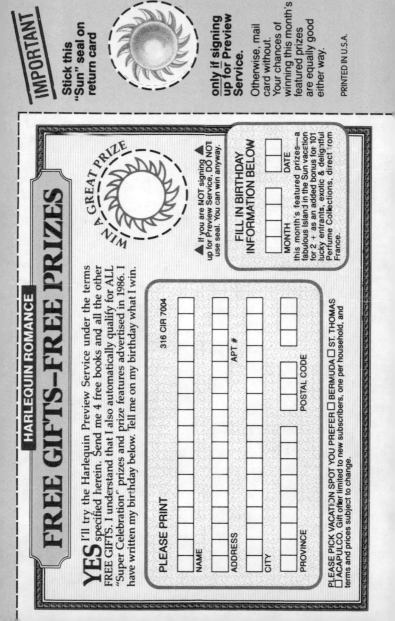

HARLEQUIN ROMANCE

FREE GIFTS—FREE PRIZES

YES I'll try the Harlequin Preview Service under the terms specified herein. Send me 4 free books and all the other FREE GIFTS. I understand that I also automatically qualify for ALL "Super Celebration" prizes and prize features advertised in 1986. I have written my birthday below. Tell me on my birthday what I win.

WIN ▲ GREAT PRIZE

◀ If you are NOT signing up for Preview Service, DO NOT use seal. You can win anyway.

FILL IN BIRTHDAY INFORMATION BELOW

MONTH		DATE

this month's featured prizes—a fabulous Island in the Sun vacation for 2 + as an added bonus for 101 lucky entrants, exotic & delightful Perfume Collections, direct from France.

PLEASE PRINT

316 CIR 7004

NAME

ADDRESS   APT #

CITY   POSTAL CODE

PROVINCE

PLEASE PICK VACATION SPOT YOU PREFER ☐ BERMUDA ☐ ST. THOMAS ☐ ACAPULCO. Gift offer limited to new subscribers, one per household, and terms and prices subject to change.

If card is missing writ
Harlequin
"Super Celebration"
Sweepstakes
P.O. Box 2800,
5170 Yonge Street
Postal Station A
Willowdale, Ontario
M2N 6J3

Harlequin
"Super Celebration" Sweepstakes
P.O. Box 2800, 5170 Yonge Street
Postal Station A
Willowdale, Ontario
M2N 6J3

PLACE
1ST CLASS
STAMP
HERE

me again and you'll regret it for the rest of your life—understand?'

'Perfectly.' Nick's unemotional response incensed Erin.

'Is that all you have to say?'

The blue eyes that swung up to her face were as cold and unfathomable as the sea on a winter's night. The angles of Nick's face seemed sharper than ever and his mouth was just a thin, hard line. If ever the devil took a physical form, Erin thought wildly, then surely he must look as Nick did now.

'What is there to say? I told you the truth.'

'So you did!' Erin spat the words at him. 'And I'm deeply grateful to you for your honesty—at least I now know just what sort of an animal I'm dealing with. Stay where you are!' she added hastily as Nick made a move as if to get to his feet. 'Don't come near me! It's as much as I can do to stand being in the same room as you!'

'Erin——' Nick began but to hear her name on his lips was more than she could bear.

'Don't speak to me!' she cried. 'I don't want to hear anything you've got to say! I wish you'd never come here! I wish you were in hell—or out there in the snow—anywhere but here!'

The living room had never appeared so warmly welcoming. The curtains had been drawn, shutting out the night, and the fire cast a rosy glow over everything, but Erin's pleasure in the sight was tainted when, pushing aside her empty plate, she turned her head and her eyes met Nick's.

He looked desperately tired, she admitted unwillingly, his eyes dimmed by the aching fatigue that came from mental strain rather than physical activity. Not that he let it show in his actions of course, he had insisted on taking his share of the household chores—washing up, fetching fresh coal—though Erin was well aware of the small signs that betrayed the way the injury to his head was still paining him. The level of the tablets in the aspirin bottle had dropped revealingly and that, combined with the lack of colour in his face and the awkward, uncomfortable way he held his head, had forced her, reluctantly, to offer to bathe the cut once more. To her relief the offer had been peremptorily refused. She had had to make it but she doubted that either of them would have found the experience a particularly comfortable one.

What little conversation there had been had been kept on a level of constrained politeness. They treated each other warily, like a pair of hostile cats circling slowly, neither of them prepared to make the first move either of conciliation or open aggression, and when Nick had stated firmly that he would prepare the evening meal Erin had neither the strength nor the inclination to argue.

Now, however, strengthened by the savoury food, and with the warmth of the fire easing some of the icy numbness that had enclosed her all afternoon, Erin felt she should at least show some appreciation of his efforts, make some pretence of civil behaviour.

'That was very good,' she said stiffly, her voice sounding distinctly odd even in her own ears.

Nick's hard mouth curved into a half-smile.

'One thing I have not forgotten is how to read. I managed to follow the recipe, but I'm no cook—so you can cross that off your list of possible occupations, along with the sergeant-major. Two down, only another few thousand to go,' he added drily. 'And when we've played guess my occupation then what will we do?'

Urged on by some malevolent little voice inside her head, Erin met his eyes directly, her expression innocent.

'Perhaps we could play at guessing your wife's name,' she suggested sweetly.

She saw the amusement fade from Nick's face, the sudden darkening of his eyes and was surprised at how hollow a triumph it was to know that she had got through to him and touched him on the raw. She had seen an opportunity to be revenged for the hurt she had suffered at his hands and had taken it unthinkingly, but it gave her no pleasure to realise that she had succeeded in hurting him in return.

'You really know how to put the knife in, don't you?' Nick said softly. 'But why stop there, Erin? Why not guess the little boy's name as well? Surely you haven't forgotten there was a child in the photograph too?'

Erin winced at the bitterness of Nick's tone. Already she was regretting her childish urge to hit back, the recurring doubts she had had as to the reality of Nick's loss of memory fading before the raw emotion on his face.

'Nick—don't!' she begged miserably.

'What's the matter, Erin?' The silky menace in Nick's voice sent an icy shiver down Erin's spine. 'Revenge not as sweet as it's made out to be?'

'No.' Erin shook her head vehemently. 'No it's not—and I'm sorry! I should never have said that, it was stupid and cruel. I can't think what made me say it.'

'Perhaps you're learning,' Nick responded cryptically, some of the savage cynicism leaving his voice. 'If it makes you feel any better, I was expecting something like this. We can't go on avoiding the subject of the photograph, pretending that my—my——'

Suddenly, shockingly, Nick was stumbling over his words. The clear blue eyes clouded, taking on a dazed, unfocused look as he lifted a hand to shield them from the light. He looked like a man who was only half awake and struggling to free himself from some appalling dream.

CHAPTER SEVEN

ERIN sat as if frozen in her chair, hardly daring to breathe. She sensed intuitively that the mention of his wife had triggered off some echo of memory in Nick's mind just as, she now realised, something he or she had said had done this morning. What was it they had been talking about? The freezer? No, it had been when Nick had mentioned the television that he had reacted. There had to be some connection there with the terrifying confrontation over the radio but for the life of her she couldn't see what. Her mind was swinging rapidly between hope and fear; hope because Nick's reaction meant that there were some tenuous links with his past, that he had some chance of remembering, and fear of the desolation that would follow if he failed.

And what about you? an insidious little voice whispered in her mind, reminding her that if Nick's memory returned he would remember his wife and child and go to them and she would lose him. Angrily Erin shook her head. There was nothing for her to lose! Nick had turned to her in a moment of despair, wanting only contact with another human being, nothing more.

Too late she remembered the man sitting opposite her. Slight as it was, her movement had been enough to catch Nick's eye, distracting him. With a sinking heart Erin saw the way his head jerked round, his eyes blurred with angry confusion. She heard him swear softly and savagely, releasing his frustration in a stream of violent curses, and she could only wait until his anger burned itself out.

Abruptly Nick got to his feet as if he could not bear to be still. Erin watched uneasily as he moved to the sideboard, snatching up the bottle of brandy he had found in his bag that morning.

'I need a drink,' he said, his voice not yet fully under control. 'Do you want one?'

'No—but——' Erin glanced worriedly at Nick's almost untouched plate. 'Do you think you should? You've hardly eaten a thing and——'

'Get off my back, Erin.' The words came softly but tinged with a deadly menace. 'I'll go to hell in my own way and I'll thank you not to interfere.'

'Nick, don't!' Erin tried again as he splashed an extravagant amount of the golden liquid into a glass.

'Nick, don't!' Nick mimicked savagely, lifting the glass in a gesture that was half salute, half threat. 'Keep out of my life, lady,' he warned. 'What there is of it is mine, and if I want to drink myself into oblivion it's no concern of yours.'

Hurt and resentment at the way he had once more excluded her made Erin's temper flare.

'I couldn't agree more!' she declared furiously, getting to her feet and collecting the plates, banging them one on top of the other carelessly, refusing to let the pain get a grip on her.

She already knew she meant nothing to him, she told herself angrily. She should have expected this.

'I'll leave you to it!' she told Nick coldly.

'That suits me fine,' he muttered, his eyes defying her to protest as he drained the last of his brandy.

As Nick turned to refill his glass Erin hesitated, her anger evaporating as swiftly as it had come. She was quite sure Nick should not be drinking like this, especially if he was still suffering from concussion, but in this mood he was quite capable of using force if she tried to take the bottle from him and, shivering in recollection of the moment he had taken the radio from her, Erin knew that she had already had enough experience of his undeniable physical strength to make her think more than twice about risking a repeat performance.

'I thought you were going to leave me in peace.' Nick's goading voice broke in on Erin's thoughts.

'Peace isn't exactly the word!' she flashed back. 'I think you were closer with the hell you mentioned earlier. And I'll go when I'm ready. This is my house, remember.'

'Could I ever forget! Why don't you draw up an account of what I owe you for board and lodging and I'll settle up when I leave—always supposing I have any money of course.'

The words stung sharply like the lash of a whip but Erin was more sensitive now to the small, tell-tale signs he couldn't quite hide. She recognised the bitter flippancy as Nick's private defence mechanism, used when things came too close, got too painful. She saw the white knuckles on the hand clenched around his glass, the bleak emptiness of his eyes, and her heart turned over in pity.

It would have been so much easier if she could have left him a few seconds earlier, not seeing, and so stayed angry, but she seemed fated to have to contend with conflicting feelings where this man was concerned.

'Get out and leave me alone,' Nick muttered through clenched teeth.

'Nick——'

'Out!' Nick repeated implacably, the look in his eyes promising a savage retribution if she did not obey him.

'I'm going,' Erin declared hastily. If he wouldn't let her near him there was nothing she could do. It was as if an earthquake had torn the room apart and she and Nick were on opposite sides of a great yawning chasm.

'If you want to destroy yourself that's your business,' she added, making one last attempt to shock Nick into sanity. 'Just don't expect me to pick up the pieces in the morning.'

She picked up the plates and walked towards the door. She was almost out of the room when Nick moved suddenly, snatching hold of her arm and jerking her back towards him.

'No!'

There was a terrible violence in his voice, the single syllable a cry of pain or despair, and his eyes looked stunned, bruised, as if he had just been hit very hard.

'For God's sake, Erin, don't go,' Nick whispered. 'Stay and talk to me—please.'

As Erin stood frozen by indecision, torn between a desire to stay and a more rational feeling that it would be far safer if she shook off his hand and went as quickly as possible, Nick took the plates from her unresisting grasp and put them and his brandy glass down on the sideboard. Then, turning her gently towards him, he took both of her hands in his, holding them lightly, almost tentatively, as if he was afraid she would repulse him violently, and his grip was not quite steady.

'Forgive me,' he said huskily. 'I didn't know what I was saying, I must have been out of my mind. For a second I touched something about myself then it blew up in my face and I'm afraid you got caught in the crossfire. I didn't mean any of it, I swear it.'

'You sounded as if you hated me.' Erin's voice was just a thread of sound and she kept her eyes fixed on the floor, not trusting herself to look at Nick. He had let her come one step nearer, opened the door just a tiny crack, and the sudden rush of feeling told her just how much that meant.

'Not you, Erin. I couldn't hate you. I think I hated myself quite a lot—and this whole damn mess I've involved you in. I thought I could handle it on my own; you've got problems enough just having me here, but when I saw you walk towards that door I knew I couldn't bear to be alone with the emptiness any more.'

At last Erin found the strength to raise her eyes to Nick's and having done so she found she could not look away again. She had seen enough of his stubborn determination not to show any weakness to guess what the confession had cost him. There was no sign now of that rigidly controlled mask or the dangerously frightening man she had seen on several occasions, there was only a confused, hurt, and very vulnerable man who had admitted at last that he needed her.

Something had happened between them, something that touched the very foundations of their relationship and lifted it on to a totally new level. Erin felt wonderfully elated and yet serenely calm. It was as if she had planted the seed of some very beautiful flower, a fragile blossom that would need time and care to come to its full perfection, and she was content to wait and watch it grow. She felt that in the end it would be worth all the effort.

'I never meant to hurt you,' Nick groaned. 'I'm so sorry, Erin, more sorry than you'll ever know. Please say that you'll forgive me.'

'Forgiven and forgotten,' Erin assured him with a tender sincerity, and knew that she did not just mean their fight of a few moments before.

Nick bent his head as if he would have kissed her, his eyes fixed on her mouth, but then he hesitated as if remembering her earlier angry words and Erin knew a swift pang of disappointment. She wanted to put her arms around his neck and draw his head down to hers to seal the new understanding between them with her own kiss but even as she made a move to do just that she knew she had hesitated a second too long and the moment had gone. Nick was moving away, still keeping her hand in his, drawing her back to her chair by the fire and taking up his now familiar position opposite.

'Tell me about yourself,' he said slowly, unable in spite of all his determination to inject any life into his voice. He looked like a man who had touched hell and still carried the shadow of that horror with him and, although his tone was once more rigidly controlled, Erin knew that, this time, the barriers he had built up were not against her but a protection from his own thoughts.

'What do you want to know?' she asked hesitantly.

Talk to me, he had said, and she couldn't tell if he really wanted to know or had asked simply because listening to her would fill the black emptiness for a time.

'I want to know all about you. I feel as if you're part of my life, as if you've always been there, and yet I know as little about you as I do about myself.'

Surprisingly, once she had started Erin found that the words poured out easily. She told Nick of her training at art college, her dream of becoming a freelance knitwear designer, a dream that had seemed impossible until she had found out about her great aunt's legacy of the cottage and enough money to live on for a year or two until she got started. In response to his questions she explained that she was an only child, her voice faltering slightly as she touched on her mother's death when she was twelve. She would have stopped there but his gentle, sensitive questioning drew her out until she found she was telling him just how much she missed the understanding support and advice only a mother could give.

Nick never pushed her further than she wanted to go but in response to his quiet, perceptive comments Erin found it easy to be completely frank in admitting just how hard she had found it when her father had married for the second time, five years after her mother's death.

'Elaine—that's my stepmother—and I didn't take to each other. The marriage is no great love match; Dad was lonely and Elaine wanted someone to support her, give her material comforts, so it's an arrangement that suits them both—but it wouldn't do for me.'

'And what would suit you?' Nick asked. 'You've told me about your ambitions, but are you just a career girl? I find it hard to believe that an attractive girl like you has no man in her life—other than the imaginary Rufus of course.'

'There was someone,' Erin said slowly, trying to picture Geoff's face in her mind.

But the image refused to form. She could remember separate details but they would not coalesce into a whole and when she closed her eyes in concentration it was Nick's face that floated before her, clear and vividly alive so that she blinked hastily in shock.

'Was?' Nick questioned softly.

'He married someone else.'

Erin's voice shook slightly as she answered. She felt bewildered by the speed and clarity with which Nick's face had come into her mind when she had wanted to think of Geoff, and her own feelings, or rather lack of them, added to her confusion. She had always assumed that her long-standing relationship with Geoff would lead to marriage, although nothing had been said to put things on a more formal footing, so she had been devastated when Geoff had told her of his love for Becky. At the time she had thought that nothing could ever hurt her more but now there was no pain, not even a mild regret.

'Had you known him long?'

'Years. He joined our family doctor's practice just before Dad married again.' A smile touched Erin's lips at the memory of how Geoff's quiet, steady presence had helped her through that difficult time.

'And you loved him.' It was a statement, not a question. 'But he didn't love you. I see,' Nick said flatly.

But you don't see! Erin wanted to protest, because at last she was able to think of Geoff clearly, without her own hurt pride clouding the issue. She could see now that she had loved him—and still loved him—but as a sister loves an admired older brother, nothing more. It was as if the last of the chains that bound her to the past had suddenly snapped and fallen away and an exhilarating sense of freedom and renewal shot through her.

'There'll be someone else.' Nick's voice sounded distant as if he had taken several steps away from her. 'You're very young yet. How old *are* you, Erin? Nineteen? Twenty?'

'I'm nearly twenty-three!' Erin protested.

'You don't look it—and mentally you're still a child—a real innocent.'

'And you know it all I suppose!' Erin declared satirically, her temper coming to boil again which was all the more disturbing when normally she considered herself to be a reasonably even-tempered person. The violent fluctuations of mood she had experienced in the past twenty-four hours were not at all characteristic of the person she thought she was.' After all, thirty-three, is so very old!'

Nick's mouth twisted wryly.

'I sincerely hope not,' he murmured. 'But physical age has nothing to do with it. There's so much in this world that doesn't touch you,' he went on, his voice sharpening noticeably. 'You live such a sheltered existence here in your cottage with your pretty designs and your patchwork—but you damn well don't know the half of it and that's what makes you such an innocent.'

As Nick spoke Erin stared at him bemusedly. Nothing in what had gone before could have provoked this sudden outburst! It was the radio incident all over again but in a different way. It was as if she had somehow pressed a switch and the words had started to flow automatically. Erin felt a cold, prickling sensation as if the hairs on the back of her neck were lifting in apprehension, for Nick's voice held a ring of conviction, a depth of certainty that could only have come from some knowledge or experience in the time he could not remember.

'I'm not blind, Nick,' she said gently, controlling her voice so that no hint of her rising excitement betrayed her. 'I know there's so much suffering in the world, so many wars; no one can close their eyes to such things—especially not at Christmas time.'

'Peace on Earth, goodwill to all men,' Nick quoted with savage cynicism. 'But you don't know what war's like, Erin; how can you, sitting here so safe and secure! You might read newspaper reports with everything carefully cleaned up and toned down so that it's bearable, but someone once said that the first casualty of war is the truth and—Godammit, Erin!—you don't know the first thing about the truth!'

Erin's lips felt dry and she wetted them nervously before she tried to speak again. No wonder Nick had reacted so strongly to her teasing comment about the army! She had touched on something that went very deep, something so intrinsically a part of him that she could have no doubt he was speaking from first-hand experience. But when? Where?

Erin was no longer afraid she might hear something destructive to her own peace of mind. The way Nick had picked up her mention of war, the bitterness and revulsion in his voice when he spoke of it, told her that he was not by nature a man of violence. The conviction was growing in her that he had switched off the radio so swiftly because, subconsciously, *he* could not bear to hear the reports he had said might depress *her*.

Could she risk pushing him any further? She had no knowledge of such things and was very much afraid of the consequences for Nick if she probed too deeply, but there was nothing in what he said that told her *why* he felt as he did and what appalling memory lay buried in his forgotten past. A few minutes more and she was convinced he would remember.

'Tell me about the truth, Nick,' she said quietly.

At once she knew she had gone too far. Nick's head jerked back, his eyes narrowing swiftly, but not before Erin had seen the flicker of violent emotion that was ruthlessly suppressed before he spoke.

'What are you up to, Erin?' he asked sharply.

Erin could have wept with disappointment. She had been so close to a breakthrough! But she had rushed it, blundering blindly in a situation in which she was out of her depth, and once more Nick had moved away from her, his defences coming up again. Her hands clenched into tight fists, shaking with frustration. She couldn't stop now!

'Is this why you don't want to listen to the news? Because you know what war's really like, because——'

She broke off abruptly as Nick's hands came up before his face in an instinctive defensive gesture.

'No more!' he said shakily. 'Stop it—now!'

'But——'

'Stop it, Erin! Don't play psychiatrist, for God's sake! You don't know what you're doing!'

'But Nick, if you think about what you said——' Erin had to force herself to ignore the torment in Nick's eyes and go on. 'If you try to remember, I'm sure you will! It's all there, just below the surface, and——'

'Erin, that's enough! I can't face any more, not tonight.'

Nick did not raise his voice but the lines etched into his face, the grey pallor of his skin, reinforced his words as no violent tone ever could. Immediately Erin was filled with contrition. In her excitement she had made no allowances for what Nick had already been through that night and the after-effects of the injury to his head. She knew she could risk no further questioning. Nick was on the edge of a precipice as it was; one mistake on her part could push him over.

But she could still think. All that had happened gave her some hope that Nick's loss of memory was not permanent and if she pieced together all the tiny fragments of evidence she might begin to see a picture.

Erin didn't question why it was so important to her to do so, important in a way that went far beyond the need to discover who Nick was for the sake of her own peace of mind. In just one short day Nick had become so much a part of her life that she couldn't imagine how it had felt not to know him. It was dangerous, it went against every law of common sense, and it was possibly the worst thing that could happen to her but it had happened and all the rational argument in the world couldn't change it.

CHAPTER EIGHT

ERIN'S pencil flew over the paper. She had not felt so satisfied with anything she had done for a long time. These designs were *good*! Without arrogance she knew they were some of the best she had ever produced and her fingers itched to make them up on her knitting machine to see if the finished product matched up to her mental image of it. She was so caught up in her own private world that she started violently when Nick came to her side.

'I was going to make some tea,' he said brusquely. 'Want some?'

Erin watched him go out of the room, a disturbed frown clouding her face. When Nick had insisted that she carry on with her work as if he wasn't there she had doubted that it would be possible. She had always preferred to be alone when she worked, finding anyone—even Geoff—a distraction. But Nick had been so still and silent that she had hardly noticed that he was in the room.

Her frown deepened. Nick had been unnervingly distant and preoccupied all day. He had left her abruptly last night, making no effort to hide his exhaustion, but today he had seemed better, physically at least. There had been no recurrence of the weakness that had frightened her yesterday, but she had no idea of his mental state and Nick did not seem prepared to enlighten her. It was as if the openness between them had never been, or perhaps he felt that he had given too much of himself away, revealed a vulnerability he hadn't wanted her to see, so that now he had withdrawn from her again. Being with him was like

113

riding a roller-coaster, reaching up to something like
communication one minute, only to plunge down
again with unnerving speed the next. Ostensibly he
had been reading for the last three hours, but Erin
doubted if she had heard a page turn more than twice
in all that time.

The long silent day had given her too much time to
think, to reconsider all her doubts and fears, balancing
her intuitive feelings of the night before against the fact
that she had no concrete evidence to support her
instincts. Erin didn't know what to think any more; if
anything, she felt further from a solution now than on
the day of Nick's arrival.

Abandoning her futile attempt to come to any
conclusion, Erin was back at work when Nick returned,
her head bent over the drawing board, and he placed
the mug of tea near her without speaking. She thought
he had moved away again and so was startled when she
felt a light touch on her hair at the nape of her neck.
Gently Nick moved the brown curls aside then bent his
head and kissed her very softly, his lips warm on the
delicate skin.

Erin's pencil stilled instantly and her fingers tightened
round it, her eyes closing so that she could better enjoy
the entrancing sensations that set her body tingling in
response to the featherlight caress, but the whisper of
cold air across her skin as Nick lifted his head again
brought her back down to earth and she tensed
immediately.

'Don't!' she gasped protestingly.

She sensed the tautness of the dark figure at her back
and could not bring herself to turn and meet those cold
blue eyes. One lean brown hand lingered on her neck
and Erin's mouth was suddenly dry at the thought of
the strength in those long fingers, imagining the ease
with which they could move ever so slightly to close
over her throat. Out of the corner of her eye she saw

Nick's hand clench tightly then abruptly it was snatched away.

'My apologies.' Nick's voice was coldly formal. 'I forgot you didn't like to be touched. It won't happen again.'

Then he was gone, flinging himself down in his chair and picking up his book once more, holding it before him like a barrier.

Slowly Erin lifted her pencil to continue with her drawing then stopped, the point still hovering inches above the paper. Her concentration had vanished completely, evaporating in the fiery heat that had flooded through her veins at the touch of Nick's lips. She couldn't even remember what she had been thinking in the seconds before he had kissed her.

What was happening to her? She knew her feelings for Nick were purely sexual, knew how dangerous it would be to give in to them, but he had only to touch her and what little detachment she had achieved fled, leaving her frighteningly susceptible to the lightest caress.

Erin's eyes slid to the silent figure in the chair by the fire, her gaze lingering on the powerful lines of Nick's body, the muscular length of his legs so clearly defined in the tight-fitting black jeans, and she knew with a painful, heart-stopping certainty that if a sudden and very rapid thaw did not put an end to their enforced isolation soon she would let Nick make love to her.

Somehow the realisation did not shock her as she might have expected it would. She accepted it as one would have to accept the inevitable—and it was inevitable. It followed as naturally from her feelings as one breath follows another. What disturbed and bewildered her was the unanswerable question—why Nick?

She knew that all she should feel towards him was fear and distrust and she had certainly experienced both those emotions. The memory of the moment he had forced her to pull a knife on him haunted her dreams. But, try as she might, she couldn't bring herself to fear him *enough* to overcome those other feelings that, against every law of sanity and self-preservation, threatened to swamp her completely.

Why this man more than any other? How could he make the ground feel insubstantial beneath her feet until she thought it might crumble away beneath her, sending her spiralling into the vast chasm of the unknown? In admitting that she couldn't answer that, Erin knew she was also admitting that if—when—Nick did make love to her she was risking a savage and total destruction of her peace of mind. And yet she knew, without hope of salvation, that if he did not then the results would be equally devastating.

Nick himself had warned her of the dangers of their enforced intimacy, she remembered miserably. 'We have no future, you and I,' he had told her and, rationally, she knew he was right—but when he touched her she didn't think rationally!

Erin had never thought of herself as someone who was prepared to settle for just the present. The loss of her mother had left a gap in her life, one she had dreamed of filling with a strong and lasting love of her own, and her father's second-best marriage to Elaine had reinforced that ideal. She had had hopes of such a love with Geoff, with him she had been prepared to wait and work towards a future, but with Nick she had no thought of waiting, no thought of anything beyond today.The problem fretted at Erin's mind and she was no closer to solving it when, after an uncomfortably silent meal, she sat huddled near to the fire, letting the golden flicker of the flames soothe her with their hypnotic effect.

'What's this? Another of your great aunt's antiques?' Nick's voice jolted her out of her trance and she struggled to focus her gaze on the polished oak box he held.

'Yes, that was Aunt Bee's. It's a backgammon board,' she said and was relieved to find that her voice was strong, with none of the tremor she had feared might betray her when she tried to speak. 'It's been in the family for generations, it's over a hundred years old.'

'There's an inscription on the lid,' Nick went on, 'but I'm afraid my Latin's not up to a translation. Do you know what it means?'

'Aunt Bee did tell me.' Erin frowned thoughtfully, trying to remember. 'Oh yes, I've got it now—"As in life, so in a game of hazard, skill will make something of the worst of throws." '

There was a loud crash as the box fell from Nick's hands and landed heavily on the floor, scattering its contents. Nick swung away suddenly as the carved wooden men went flying and one of them landed beside Erin's foot. With an exclamation of annoyance she snatched it up.

'Why can't you be more careful!' she exclaimed angrily, jumping up and hurrying to retrieve the box from the floor. 'I told you this was very old, you might have damaged it with your carelessness! Well don't just stand there! You could at least help me pick things up! Are you listening to me, Nick? Nick?'

Erin's tirade ceased in mid-flow as she glanced in Nick's direction. Her anger fled, replaced by a fearful clenching of her stomach as she saw how he stood swaying unsteadily, his hands pressed tight against his temples, his face contorted with pain.

'Oh God! Nick, what is it?'

She was at his side in a second, clutching at his arm, but he muttered something unintelligible and wrenched himself away from her, slumping down on the settee, his breathing harsh and uneven.

'Nick——'

Erin took a hesitant step towards him then froze, terrified by his sudden violent withdrawl. The tension in every muscle in his body, the way he sat hunched forwards as if in pain, the unrelenting pressure of his hands against his head, all warned her to stay away. At that moment his isolation was complete and she knew he would turn savagely on anyone who tried to intrude on the intensely private world that had reached out so suddenly to enclose him.

But she couldn't leave him to suffer like this, she had to try to reach him so that he knew he wasn't entirely alone. She had no idea how to help him, she only knew she had to try.

Erin's heart seemed to be beating high up in her throat as she knelt on the floor at Nick's side but her mind was suddenly calm as she concentrated all her thoughts on the man before her, crushing down her instinctive longing to put her arms round him. She couldn't touch him yet, any physical contact might startle him and a shock could be dangerous. She had rushed it before and ruined things by doing so, she must be more careful this time. Clasping her hands nervously in her lap, clenching them until her knuckles showed white, she forced herself to speak slowly and clearly.

'Nick, can you hear me? You're not alone, I'm here and I want to help.'

There was no response from the still figure on the settee and Erin bit her lips hard in anxiety and disappointment. She wasn't getting through to him; she doubted if he was even aware of her existence.

'Nick,' she tried again. 'Please listen. Please let me help you.'

Nick muttered a savage curse, his voice rough and thick, terrifying Erin with its ferocity, but at least it was a response.

'Can you tell me what happened?'

The mumbled reply was scarcely intelligible. Erin caught the word 'name', nothing more.

'What name?' she questioned, the erratic pounding of her heart making the words come out in a breathless gasp. 'Do you mean *your* name?'

Suddenly Nick's eyes flew open to stare sightlessly straight in front of him. He looked as if he was trying to focus on something far, far away.

'My name,' he said hoarsely and Erin's heart twisted painfully at the effort it cost him to speak.

Did she dare to ask the question that was on the tip of her tongue? Twice Erin tried to speak and both times her nerve failed her. On the third attempt she was more successful though her voice croaked embarrassingly.

'What is your name?'

The silence that followed her question seemed to stretch endlessly on and on. Erin found she was holding her breath and, without realising it, she crossed her fingers superstitiously in her lap.

'Hazard—Nick—Hazard.'

The words came painfully slowly. The name meant nothing to Erin. If she had heard it, even with only half her mind, as the name of a wanted man then surely she would remember? With a bewildering swiftness Nick's mood seemed to change. His head came up, the arrogant, defiant set to his jaw oddly at variance with the way his dark, unfocused eyes seemed to look straight through Erin, as if he could see some other, invisible person standing behind her.

'And that's all I'm going to tell you,' he said harshly.

Reacting purely instinctively, Erin put her hand on Nick's arm. She had no idea what he was thinking but at least he was responding and the last few words, strange as they had been, had been uttered in a voice that was strong and firm.

'That's all right, Nick,' she assured him. 'You don't have to tell me anything you don't want.'

Light as it was, the touch of her hand on his arm made Nick start violently. He glanced down at her fingers resting on the grey wool of his sleeve then his eyes swung up to her face, clearer now but with a puzzled, wary frown creasing the space between his brows.

'Who the hell are you?' he demanded roughly.

The question was so unexpected that Erin rocked back on her heels, one hand going to her mouth to still the cry of shock that rose to her lips. The cold hostility in Nick's eyes made her want to spring to her feet and run, seeking the sanctuary of her room. She had a sudden vivid mental picture of the moment she had pulled the knife on Nick and the ease with which he had disarmed her, and her whole body became rigid with fear.

'Who——' Nick began menacingly and the single syllable was enough to jolt her into speech.

'I'm Erin, Nick—*Erin*—you must remember me!'

'Erin?' Nick repeated her name dully, shaking his head as if he had never heard it before. 'No—not Erin.' His expression changed suddenly, his eyes anxiously questioning. 'Where's Marie?' he asked urgently.

Even as Erin's mouth opened in shock a germ of an idea was growing in her mind. In his thoughts Nick was not `here, at Moor End Cottage with her, but somewhere he had known before he lost his memory. He was living in his past!

'There's no Marie here,' she said carefully. 'There's just me. Who is Marie? Your wife?'

The look Nick turned on her was one of scathing contempt.

'Don't be bloody stupid!' he snarled. 'I don't have a wife! Would I be in a hell on earth like this if I was married?' There was no time to think, no time to do more than register what he had said, before Nick went on, 'But Marie—what about . . .'

Nick's voice trailed off and his eyelids drooped in sudden exhaustion. With an effort that was painful to watch he forced them open again.

'Who did you say you were?' he asked drearily, slurring the words slightly.

The dazed, confused look that had come to his face gave Nick an air of vulnerability that made Erin's heart ache in sympathy. She caught hold of his hand, folding both of her own around it and gripping tightly.

'I'm Erin.' She spoke slowly and emphatically. 'Erin Haworth. And this is Moor End Cottage. Don't you remember? We've been snowed in for days.'

Shakily Nick's hand came up before his face as if to ward off some blow. Then, just as Erin felt she might weep with despair, he shook his head slightly and with a sob of relief she saw the dull, blank look leave his eyes and knew that he could see her, really see her, at last.

'Erin?' he said huskily and it was Nick who spoke, not the frightening stranger who had been with her before.

'You know me!' Erin exclaimed, half laughing, half crying in her delight.

'Of course I know you!' Nick's tone was sharp but then he studied Erin's face more closely, taking in her lack of colour, the way her eyes were still unnaturally wide with fear and anxiety. 'Dear God, Erin,' he whispered. 'What happened?'

'You remembered,' Erin told him gently. 'Or, rather, you went back into the past. You lost yourself, you were somewhere else, in another time.' Erin shivered at the memory. 'It was horrible but it's over now. You're safe; you're back here with me.'

Then, simply because it seemed the right thing to do, as a gesture offering comfort to someone in need, she leaned forward and kissed Nick gently on his mouth. She was unprepared for the speed and strength with which he responded, gathering her up in his arms, imprisoning her when she would have moved away, his lips hard against hers.

Erin's mind seemed to split in two, one half of it welcoming the fierce passion of Nick's kiss, the other rejecting it desperately, struggling against the burning sensation that threatened to overwhelm her.

Every feminine instinct in her body urged her to surrender, to submit to the elemental force that was far stronger than any rational thought. It was as if she had been born a woman for this moment, for the sole purpose of knowing this man's full possession—but she did not want it to be like this, like that first evening when he had turned to her in despair, not wanting *her* but needing any woman. When she gave herself to Nick it had to be because at that moment he wanted her more than anyone else in the world. She couldn't have his love, she couldn't even have the whole man because without his past he was only a shadow, but at least she could have that. Only then could she bear the double-edged ecstasy of having Nick make love to her.

With a muffled sigh Nick lay back against the cushions, drawing Erin up beside him, his arms curving possessively around her waist as they lay close together.

'Tell me about it,' he said unevenly. 'What did I say?'

Erin didn't know where to begin, her mind forming only incoherent, disjointed thoughts. She was too intensely aware of Nick's strong brown fingers splayed out across her ribs, his thumb resting just below the curve of her breast, so that when she tried to speak her throat closed up until she thought she would suffocate and she could only shake her head wordlessly.

'What is it?' Nick's voice was suddenly tight with suspicion. 'Is there something you're afraid to tell me?'

'No.'

'Then tell me! For God's sake, Erin——'

'Please!' Erin lifted her hand to his mouth, stilling his angry protest. 'I'll tell you everything but—it's hard.'

She felt the faint pressure of Nick's lips against her fingers before he removed her hand, absently smoothing his thumb against the soft skin as he expelled his breath in a harsh sigh.

'Take your time,' he said more calmly. 'I'm listening.'

Erin stared fixedly at their linked hands as she began speaking, her voice shaking as she relived the scene in her mind.

'You said your name was Nick Hazard,' she said and sensed Nick's faint start as he registered the name. 'And you were—edgy—hostile—as if you were in some unbearable situation and there was someone there you didn't trust. But it was more than that—you said you were in a hell on earth.'

The hand that held hers so gently clenched tightly, painfully, and Erin felt the sudden change in the steady beat of Nick's heart beneath her cheek so that she had to struggle to find the strength to go on. It hurt terribly even to recall the savage bitterness with which Nick had said those words.

'Is that all?' Nick's voice was very low and Erin shook her head slowly.

'I think there was someone else with you—a woman—but not your wife. You said you weren't married.'

'Interesting,' Nick murmured and Erin flinched inside at the ironical note in his voice. Taken at face value, that dry comment might have deceived her before, making her think he didn't care, but now she recognised it as a danger sign. 'This woman, did she have a name?'

'Marie.'

Erin glanced at Nick's face as she gave the name he had used and she saw him frown thoughtfully then shake his head.

'That means nothing to you?'

'Nothing.' The word came starkly, leaving countless other things unsaid.

'But you asked for her more than once. You sounded desperately worried about her! Who is she, Nick?'

'How the hell should I know?' Nick snarled, the mask slipping for a second, revealing the harrowed face behind it. 'I don't know any Marie! The name means damn all to me. Are you sure that's what I said?'

'I'm positive. You asked where she was—and you didn't recognise me. But of course you were remembering a time when you didn't know me.'

A hint of bitterness had crept into Erin's voice. It stung painfully to realise that there had been so much time, almost all his life, when Nick hadn't even known she existed.

'Perhaps Marie is the woman in the photograph?'

Nick would not meet Erin's questioning gaze.

'What do you think?' he countered aggressively.

'I don't know. She could be. After all, you don't have to be married to ... to ...'

'To father a child?' Nick finished for her. 'How true. Is that what I'm trying to escape from?' One dark eyebrow lifted, sardonically questioning. 'Perhaps my misspent youth had finally caught up with me.'

'Nick, be serious!' Erin pleaded, unable to bear the black, defensive humour any longer. What had happened to the openness there had been between them?

'I am serious.'

Nick's vivid blue eyes locked with Erin's softer hazel ones and held her gaze hypnotically, their colour deepening until they were as dark as a midnight sky, and Erin trembled at the hidden fires she saw burning there.

'Or at least I'm trying to be,' Nick went on huskily. 'But it's damned hard to think of anything coherently with your sexy little body pressed up against me like this. You must know what you're doing to me, Erin. I want you so much that I can't think straight any more. I can't give a damn who or what I am if I can't have you. It's driving me distracted to be with you like this, to imagine how it could be between us, but not to *know!*'

'Nick——' Erin croaked, shifting uneasily under the intensity of his gaze then wishing she hadn't when the slight movement only brought her closer up against him.

'We could be so good together,' Nick murmured, stroking his hand down the tender skin of her neck.

For a moment the long fingers rested on the spot where her pulse throbbed fiercely and the slowly sensual curve of his mouth left Erin in no doubt that he felt the pounding of her blood and knew the reason for it so that she had no hope of hiding her own arousal from him.

Nick's hands slid slowly over her body, lingering softly on the curves of her breasts and hips and Erin felt as if her bones were melting in the fires that were burning inside her. His touch was too light, too controlled, and, impatient at his restraint, she arched her back, pressing herself against his hands, needing to feel his strength, knowing that the intemperate clamouring of her senses would not be appeased by such a gentle caress. The swift increase of pressure in response set a match to the smouldering fire of her desire and she reached blindly for Nick, her fingers clenching in the dark silk of his hair as on a sigh of pure pleasure she yielded her mouth to his.

Nick moved so that he was lying half across her, the hard weight of his body pressing her down into the soft cushions, and every nerve in her body gloried in the feel of such an imprisonment. She slid her hands lower, closing them about his shoulders, crying out in protest when it seemed he would have moved away. But Nick had only shifted his position slightly to prop himself up on one elbow as he studied her face intently.

'This is only the beginning, Erin,' he murmured softly. 'God, if you knew how much I've wanted this! I've wanted you from the moment I saw you!'

His voice had deepened suddenly and the intensity with which he spoke had a force that was almost physical, so that Erin shuddered as if she could feel his words falling on her newly sensitive nerves. There was no gentleness in Nick when he captured her mouth again and she welcomed his savagery, feeling her own passion grow to match his. Her hands closed over the soft wool of his sweater, tugging it free at his waist until her fingers dug into the smooth skin of his back.

'Yes!' Nick sighed against her lips. 'Touch me, Erin! I want to feel your hands on me. I want to feel all of you, know every tiny inch of you. I *want* you—you're all I know. I need you—oh God, how I need you!'

The blood in Erin's veins turned to ice; she felt as cold as death. Her hands stiffened, paralysed against the powerful muscles of Nick's back. There was no warmth or light, only the aching, numbing cold, and in the blackness of her mind an anguished voice sobbing, 'Not like this!. . . Not like this!'

With a despairing moan Erin wrenched her mouth away from Nick's, twisting her head frantically on the cushions so that she did not have to meet his eyes. In his arms she felt as if she had touched heaven and she knew that if he had spoken one word of love—no, she hadn't even needed that—if he had left those fatal words, 'You're all I know,' unsaid, then she would have given herself to him freely and joyfully. But he had said them and in doing so had slammed the door on the heaven she reached for.

'No,' she groaned. 'No—I can't——'

Incredibly, Nick laughed.

'Liar!' he reproved softly. 'Can't doesn't come into it. There's no need for this, Erin, we both know it's just pretence.'

His hands were sliding under her sweater as he spoke, the strong fingers moving slowly and deliberately upwards towards her breasts, his touch sensuously enticing, tempting her to yield. Already her treacherous body was aching for him, almost beyond the control of her mind. In another second she would lose herself completely, abandoning herself to the sensual mastery of his hands, and the dark tide of desire would close over her head, drowning all rational thought.

But she had to think, though her body screamed in protest as she dragged herself back from the precipice over which she had almost fallen. This was not love, or even passion, it was a physical need born of despair. Nick wanted her only as some warmly willing companion, someone who would hold back the darkness for a while, ease the raw wound in his mind and help him to forget for a brief time at least that he was alone, without a past or future—and that was not enough!

'No!'

With strength born of desperation Erin pushed at Nick's chest, twisting her body out from under his. She landed on the floor with a force that jarred every bone, making her head reel sickeningly. Her mind was one nagging ache and bitter tears burned her eyes.

'What the hell are you playing at, Erin?' Nick's softly spoken words were tinged with a cold anger that penetrated the grey haze inside Erin's mind, driving away the protecting mist as an icy wind might shatter clouds, blowing them into tiny shreds, so that she sprang to her feet in a panic, drawing herself up to meet those inimical blue eyes.

'I don't——' Erin choked on the words, terrified that Nick would see them for the lie they were. '. . . I don't want you!' she finished desperately, the words echoing shrilly in the silence of the night.

'Liar.'

It was no soft reproach this time but a savage, menacing sound, all the more shocking because Nick did not raise his voice. She should be used to that ruthless control by now, she'd seen enough of it in the short time she had known Nick, but in her present situation it was the stuff of which nightmares were made.

'You're lying,' Nick repeated brutally. 'Lying to me and to yourself.'

'No!' It was a cry of despair, forced from her lips by fear though her heart threatened to break with the anguish of denying the truth.

When Nick got to his feet Erin retreated hastily, her breath coming in a shocked gasp of terror as she saw the smouldering violence that darkened his eyes.

Oh God, she'd misread everything! She had come to believe that the violence of Nick's behaviour had been only a reaction to the stress of the situation in which he found himself—she had *wanted* to believe that!—but if she had been wrong . . . One hand went to her throat in an instinctively defensive gesture.

The effect on Nick of that one small movement was dramatic. He stopped dead, the dark anger draining from his face, his eyes raw with the emotion she had glimpsed in a similar situation on that first evening.

'Dear God,' he whispered brokenly. 'What's happening to me?'

He lifted one hand in an odd, imploring gesture, not touching her, as if afraid of her response.

'Erin,' he said shakily. 'There's no need for this. I've told you how I feel——'

'So you have!'

Bitter pain made Erin's voice harsh and the hurt was made all the more unbearable as she saw the way Nick's hand was snatched back at the sound.

'You left me in no doubt on that score when you told me that you despised yourself for making love to me—

did you think I would let you put me through that again? Don't claim you *felt* anything for me, you've already told me that any woman would do! So now you know what it's like to feel as I did then—to be rejected as you rejected me!'

All colour had left Nick's face and the blue eyes had lost their vivid brightness, looking suddenly dull.

'So that's what all this is about,' he said heavily. 'I must be every kind of fool because I never suspected you were out for revenge. I actually believed you when you said that that was forgiven and forgotten.'

Erin had thought she was beyond feeling any more pain but Nick's words hit her so hard that she felt dazed and sick as if he had actually aimed a blow at her. In her anguish she too had said words that should never have been heard, angry, hurtful words that had destroyed any hope that there could ever be any trust between them, and it was too late to wish them back.

"I should have seen it coming shouldn't I?' Nick's voice was thick with savage self-derision. 'But you laid your trap so carefully didn't you, my sweet?' His tone turned the endearment into an obscenity.

Numbly Erin remained silent, her head bowed, concentrating all her energy on keeping herself upright, for her legs threatened to give way at an moment.

'Nothing to say? No,' Nick answered his own question. 'I don't suppose there is anything more to say. What you really want now is to go somewhere quiet and enjoy your twisted little triumph. Well go on—get out!'

He made a violent gesture towards the door then swung away from her, heading towards the sideboard where the bottle of brandy stood where he had left it the night before.

'Oh don't!' Erin found her voice at last and Nick turned very slowly, the bottle in his hand.

'What's this?' he taunted. 'Not remorse surely? Be

fair, Erin. You're not giving anything so why should you complain if I find my—consolation—elsewhere?'

'Nick, what are you doing to yourself?'

'Don't you know?' Nick returned sardonically, deliberately misinterpreting her question. 'I should have thought it was only too obvious. If you're wise you'll go to bed now and stay there because I intend to sit here— with this,' he lifted the brandy bottle, 'and get absolutely blind drunk. And this time nothing you do is going to stop me.'

CHAPTER NINE

THE kitchen clock was just striking three as Erin stood
in the open doorway, staring out at the bleak scene
before her. The trees stood even more starkly now
without their coating of white and the snow had sunk
down an inch or two perhaps, but no more. The
tentative fall of rain there had been earlier in the night
had done nothing to ease their situation.

The shudder that ran through her as she closed the
door had little to do with the bitter cold even though
she was wearing only her nightdress, having had to get
up because Rufus had insisted on being let out.
Thinking of the rain, she had been forced to remember
the time after she had left Nick and gone up to her
bedroom, hardly out of the living room before she
heard the chink of the bottle against the glass, and a
moment later the door was kicked to behind her with a
resounding slam that echoed throughout the silent
house.

Erin had no idea how long she had lain awake, her
overwrought mind working overtime imagining the
possible consequences for Nick if he carried out his plan
of getting drunk on top of the stress of the earlier part
of the evening. It was foolish she knew; why should she
care what happened to Nick? But she did care, she
cared more than it was safe to admit, even to herself.
Erin twisted her hands together, her nails digging into
her palms. If only she had resisted that betraying
impulse to kiss Nick in the first place, if only ... She
sighed despondently. There were too many 'if onlys'.

'You're not asleep then?'

Absorbed in her unhappy thoughts, Erin had not

heard the door opening quietly and now she turned wide, startled eyes towards Nick as he lounged in the doorway, dark and satanically threatening like some terrible demon conjured up by her reverie. Apart from a wild, unnatural glitter in his eyes he showed no sign of being drunk and his words were clear and distinct, with no hint of slurring when he spoke again.

'I saw your light was on so I thought you might like to know that your prayers have been answered. Obviously God listens to virtuous young maidens, so you've got what you wanted—it's raining.'

Automatically Erin tilted her head, listening hard. She could just make out the pattering of raindrops on the roof. The rain had come far sooner than she had expected—too soon—or did she mean too late? At least it would set Nick free.

'Will it clear the snow?' she asked unthinkingly and saw Nick's mouth twist bitterly at her question.

'Give it time, darling, it's only just begun. But keep praying and this shower might turn into a downpour— who knows, you might even be able to throw me out tomorrow.'

Something in Erin wanted to cry out in protest at what he said but she clamped her lips tight shut on the impetuous words. Nick would never believe them anyway.

'So now you have something to look forward to, don't you?' Nick taunted as he straightened up. 'That should send you off to sleep happy.'

'Go to bed, Nick, you're drunk.' Erin spoke coldly to hide the misery she was feeling.

'I should be so lucky!' was the cynical rejoinder. 'Oh, I've been drinking, I can't deny that, and I tried damned hard to get drunk—I wanted to forget.'

He laughed suddenly, a harsh, frightening sound with no humour in it that had Erin cowering back against the pillows.

'Now there's an irony—I wanted to forget! For all I know, my life only started three days ago and already I want to forget half of it. You must find that one hell of a joke!'

Erin winced at the savage satire of his tone. He had spoken the truth when he'd said he wasn't drunk. Under the influence of alcohol the barriers might have been expected to come down a little, but the black humour showed that they were still rigidly in place.

'Go to bed, Nick,' she repeated, unable to bear any more.

'Oh, I'm going,' Nick assured her. 'But just take note of one thing—I am not drunk and I remember only too clearly what happened tonight; I'm never likely to forget it. So you just keep praying, my sweet Erin, pray that the rain keeps on falling and washes the snow away. I don't think either of us would find it too pleasant to be stuck here much longer.'

Erin shook herself reprovingly. What was she doing daydreaming halfway up the stairs? She was chilled right through, her bare feet frozen. Hastily she continued on her way upstairs. She had just set foot on the landing when she heard the moaning cry from Nick's bedroom.

She froze, listening hard, catching the faint sound of movement inside the room and Nick's voice sounding blurred through the closed door. Trying to force herself to ignore it, she turned towards her own room but a second cry proved more than she could take. She was across the landing in a second but as soon as she opened Nick's door she knew she had made a grave mistake.

The light from the landing shone directly on to the bed where Nick lay on his back in a tangle of bedclothes. In spite of the cold his chest was bare and the lean, tanned body was dark against the white of the sheet. A sheen of perspiration glistened on the bronze skin and his hair was tousled and damp with sweat as it fell over his face in soft disarray.

The vulnerability of Nick's face in repose when contrasted with the powerful strength of his body was a potent force that had the effect of a blow in Erin's stomach. Even asleep, he exerted a disturbing influence over her, arousing unwanted longings so that her palms were damp with sweat, her legs unsteady beneath her. Instinct warned her that it would be safer to go now while she had the chance; she sensed that if she stayed nothing would ever be the same again. To enter Nick's room would be like leaping off that precipice into the unknown and Erin didn't know if she possessed the courage or the foolhardiness to make that move.

But as she hesitated Nick tossed restlessly on the bed, muttering incoherently, and the sound pushed Erin blindly over the edge. She ran to the bed and caught hold of his shoulder, her fingers sliding slightly on the perspiration-damp skin as she shook him gently.

'Nick, wake up! Oh, please wake up!'

Nick came awake with stunning speed, turning swiftly with a violent twisting movement and capturing Erin's hands even before his eyes were open, pinning her back against the pillows with a strength that bruised her skin, bringing a whimper of pain to her lips. Only then did his gaze go to her face, the steely blue eyes opening wide at last, filled with an expression of undisguised hostility.

'What the hell are you doing here?' he demanded harshly.

'Nick, please—you're hurting me!'

Nick lowered his eyes to where his hands held Erin's wrists captive, staring down at them as if only just becoming aware of what he had done. He released her abruptly, the aggression fading from his face as the shutters came down over it, concealing any emotion.

Impatiently he brushed a swathe of dark hair back from his forehead.

'Well, good morning, Miss Haworth,' he said with a constrained casualness. 'It is morning I take it? To what do I owe the pleasure of this little visit? Has the snow cleared already so that you can't wait to be rid of me?'

Still shocked by his sudden and violent awakening, Erin blurted out her answer with a thoughtless fervour.

'No! No, it's not like that! The snow's still there—and I wouldn't turn you out—I don't want you to go!'

'Then what are you doing here?' The hard, attacking quality had gone from Nick's voice, leaving it flat and emotionless.

'I heard you cry out. You must have been dreaming—I was worried.'

'Dreaming?' Nick sat up slowly and rubbed the back of his hand across his eyes, trying to recall the nightmare that had had him in its grip. He sighed wearily. 'God, yes,' he said heavily. 'I *was* dreaming.'

In the half-light his face was shadowed and unreadable but his voice had been totally devoid of the cynical flippancy that would have warned Erin off and in Nick that one small fact was eloquent testimony to the way he was feeling. Impulsively Erin perched on the bed beside him.

'Would it help to talk about it?' she asked diffidently. 'If you told me your dream then——' She broke off as Nick shook his head silently.

'Thanks, Erin, but no. It would only upset you—it was pretty grim—and I really don't want to talk about it.'

He reached for the packet of cigarettes that lay on the bedside table but, finding it empty, tossed it aside impatiently and Erin noticed that, for all his outwardly calm appearance, Nick's hands were not quite steady. He had rejected her offer of help but his rejection had been quiet, almost gentle, and that, taken with the absence of the black humour, gave her hope. Nick was too tired or too low to build the barriers up around himself.

'I'd like to help if I could,' she told him earnestly, not caring that her feelings showed quite openly on her face. When Nick made no response she caught hold of his hand where it lay on the bedspread. 'Please Nick! I *want* to help. If there's anything I can do——'

Very slowly Nick's free hand reached out and touched her cheek, cupping the side of her face for a moment before he let his hand drop to the bed once more. The blue eyes were strangely gentle as he searched her face, looking deep into her eyes.

'Why do you do it, Erin?' he asked softly.

Then, as Erin frowned her bewilderment, he shook his dark head in evident confusion.

'Why do you do it?' he repeated. 'Why do you take everything I throw at you and still come back for more? Don't you care about yourself? Each time I lash out at you I think, this time you've done it, this time she won't come back, no one could. Then I turn around and there you are with that crazy maternal look on your face, all concern, ready to help no matter what I do. It isn't natural! No one can forgive so much so often. So why, Erin? Why do you do it?'

Erin's first thought was that she couldn't answer him; there was no answer. Then she looked straight into Nick's face, seeing him suddenly as if she had never seen him before. She saw the ugly bruise on his forehead, the rebellious lock of hair that still fell forward despite all his efforts to brush it back. She saw those vividly blue eyes now touched with doubt and confusion, the harshly attractive features, the warm, sensual mouth, each part of his face separately and distinctly. Then all the parts fused into one and the face became Nick's again. The earth seemed to tilt once then back again, the spinning in her head stopped, and she knew with a sudden total clarity that there *was* one answer, and only one, and she was stunned to think that she hadn't known it before.

'I think it's because I love you, Nick,' she said quietly but with supreme conviction, then winced sharply as Nick's hand tightened convulsively on hers.

'Erin, no!' Nick groaned. 'For God's sake don't talk about love!'

Erin's face was white with shock, as much at the enormity of her own admission as at Nick's reaction. She didn't know how it had happened, she just knew that it had. To say the words, 'I love you', had brought a happiness such as she had never known and now that she *had* said them she knew that this was what she had been afraid of. This was the unknown, this caring for someone more than life itself, this need to be with Nick no matter what, in spite of all the doubts and fears, the angry, hurtful words that suddenly seemed so totally unimportant beside the overwhelming force of her feelings. And having faced the truth Erin knew she was no longer afraid. There was no more unknown. She loved Nick beyond thought, beyond reason, and that was all that mattered.

'Erin, you can't,' Nick was saying in a voice that was husky and unsteady. 'My sweet innocent, you can't love me.'

'But I can—I do.' Fervent sincerity rang in Erin's voice.

'But you don't know me! You only met me three days ago.'

'Time doesn't matter!' Erin protested, Geoff's words echoing in her head—and now she felt she really understood them. 'Three days, three weeks, three years, it doesn't matter! It's not a decision you make rationally, balancing for and against, it just happens. Suddenly you *know* and when you do there's no going back. That's how it is for me, Nick. I know I love you.'

'Please don't,' Nick said with sombre intensity. 'Please don't love me, Erin,' he went on hurriedly, an urgent note sharpening his voice. 'God knows, I've done nothing to deserve it and I can't take that responsibility.'

'Responsibility?' Erin echoed the word dazedly. 'Nick, what are you talking about? There's no responsibility! I love you—you don't have to do anything or be anything—you just have to accept it!'

She couldn't understand what was happening. This was not how it should be! She hadn't considered what Nick's reaction might be when she had declared her love, simply to say the words was enough—but she had never expected this!

'I love you, Nick,' she said again, but her voice trembled on the words, dying away to a whisper as she spoke his name.

Nick sighed deeply, pulling his hand from under hers to grasp her shoulders firmly.

'I can't let you love me, can't you see?' he said, shaking her slightly as he spoke. 'It would be wrong of me to take your love when I can give you nothing in return—no!' He laid a hand across Erin's mouth to silence her when she would have protested. 'Let me finish. I have nothing to give you—I can't tell you I love you, and even if I could you could never believe it. Tomorrow, the day after, whenever—if ever—my memory returns it might suddenly become a lie. I don't know who I am or what I've done and neither do you—so how can you even trust me, let alone love me?'

'But I do trust you!' Erin felt as if her world was collapsing about her. There had been so much distrust and fear but that sudden moment of realisation had wiped it all from her mind and now, with a savage irony, *Nick* was trying to put it back again. In spite of all her doubts and questions, Erin knew that, deep down, she had trusted him from the moment he had called a halt to their lovemaking—for her sake—that very first night. 'And I love the person you are. What you were, what you did, none of that matters!'

'Oh, Erin, dear child, can't you see it's all that matters?'

'Nick, don't!' Erin's eyes were bright with pain. 'Don't call me that!'

'Call you what? Dear child?' Nick's smile was gentle and touched with a world-weary resignation. 'Erin, in so many ways you are still a child. You think because you feel something for me—or think you do—then that makes everything all right. Because you care for me I won't turn out to have some sort of guilty past. But it's only in fairy tales that the frog turns out to be a prince trapped by a witch's spell, only waiting for the kiss of true love to turn him into the man he was. For both our sakes it would be rather nice to think that such things could actually happen—but this is real life, darling. Kiss this particular frog and I've got a strong suspicion he won't change at all—and certainly not into a handsome prince!'

Nick's flippancy hurt Erin more than his angry words had ever done. This time it couldn't be a defence. What was there for him to feel he had to defend himself against? She felt that he was mocking her, reducing the love she had declared for him to a mere childish infatuation. Miserably she got to her feet. Tears were pricking at her eyes but she refused to let them fall. She wanted to run from Nick and hide herself away, licking her wounds in private, but she could at least make a dignified retreat and so salvage something of her shattered pride.

'Thank you for your honesty,' she said in a high, tight voice. 'I'm sorry if I've embarrassed you by burdening you with my feelings like this; it won't happen again.'

Nick watched her silently as she turned towards the

door; she could almost feel his eyes burning into her back. Then she heard him swear under his breath and the thought that he might be cursing her stupidity broke the fragile shell she had built around herself. The tears would not be held back any longer and, blinded by them, she blundered painfully into the end of the bed.

'Erin!' Nick's shocked exclamation reached her a second before a strong, warm hand closed over her arm and she was pulled down on to the bed beside him again. 'Erin, for God's sake don't go like this!'

Nick cradled her against his side, the vital warmth of his body reaching her through the thin material of her nightdress. The temptation to rest her head on his shoulder and sob out the pain and heartbreak was almost overwhelming and Erin had to struggle in his arms, her hands pushing impotently at the hard wall of his chest.

'I have to go!' she sobbed, abandoning any attempt to restrain her tears. 'I've angered you, and if I stay I'll only make things worse.'

'Erin, you crazy child, how could I be *angry* with you?' Nick's voice changed suddenly, becoming sharp with concern. 'Sweetheart, you're frozen. Come here——'

He flung back the bedclothes, heedless of his own nakedness, and Erin had a blinding glimpse of his tightly muscled chest, rough with dark hair, a tapered waist and narrow hips and long powerful legs. Her own chest felt tight, the pounding of her heart seeming unnaturally loud in her ears.

'Nick, no!' She tried to protest, but already it was too late. Nick pulled her irresistibly down beside him, covering them both with the blankets, hiding that magnificent body from her so that Erin didn't know whether to be relieved or disappointed.

'That's better,' he murmured softly, sliding an arm

around her, curving her up against him. 'Don't worry, sweetheart, I'll soon warm you up.'

Erin could not prevent the shiver of response that shook her as she felt the hard length of Nick's body lying so close to hers. She should never have let this happen! She should have resisted, fought him, as soon as it became clear what he intended. Even now she could still do something—push him away, get out of the bed—but once more her body refused to obey her and she couldn't move. The warmth from Nick's body was slowly seeping into every pore of her skin, filling her with a drowsy contentment so that she relaxed against him, her mind drained of any thought beyond the pleasure of being held in his arms.

'That's much better,' Nick repeated, his voice as soft as a caress. 'Rule number one: never try to seduce a woman in an unheated room; cold is a real passion-killer.'

The warmth in his voice didn't fit with the teasing words. She still couldn't gauge accurately when the flippancy was real and when it was assumed. Erin tilted her head so that she could look up into the darkness of his eyes, trying to read the answer there.

'Is that what you have in mind?' she whispered. 'Were you planning to seduce me?'

Nick's grip tightened at her words and his voice was taut when he answered.

'Right now I can think of nothing I'd like more in the whole world—so don't tempt me.'

Erin's breath caught in her throat. It was as much as she could ask for and anyway she was far beyond asking for any more than that he should hold her and want her. An ache of longing suffused her body and she ran her fingers teasingly across Nick's chest, her heart lifting with his indrawn breath.

'And what if I did tempt you?' she murmured archly.

'Then you'd be answerable for the consequences,' was the gruff response.

'That seems fair.'

With only her feelings to guide her actions, Erin nestled closer, letting her fingers wander where they would, and, at first, Nick made no move to stop her. But when her hand slid lower, moving underneath the blankets, he moved swiftly, his strong fingers closing tightly around her wrist.

'None of that!' he ordered. 'Behave yourself!'

'But you said——'

'I know damn well what I said, but you weren't supposed to act on it! Erin, there's something I have to know.'

The subtle change in Nick's voice made her suddenly afraid to meet his eyes but his hand came under her chin, tilting her face up to his, subjecting it to a searching scrutiny that made her heart flutter apprehensively.

'Have you ever really known a man, Erin, in the fullest sense I mean? Have you ever made love with anyone or are you still an innocent in that way too? I want the truth, I shall know if you lie.'

Erin's eyes slid away from Nick's. She stared down at her hands still lying on the tanned skin of his chest and moved them back and forth in a restless, uneasy little gesture. She could guess what his reaction might be if she told him—and she didn't want that.

'I——' she began but Nick broke in on her.

'Too late, Erin,' he said firmly. 'I knew the answer as soon as you hesitated. You are a virgin aren't you?'

'What difference does it make?' Erin countered with soft petulance.

'It makes one hell of a difference,' Nick stated flatly. 'And if you can't see that you're more naïve than I ever dreamed. Go to sleep, Erin.'

'Sleep! But Nick——'

'But Nick, nothing! Give me patience,' Nick groaned. 'Erin, you are not making this easy for me. I can only keep on saying no for just so long.'

'Then don't say no,' Erin murmured, her lips against his chest.

She felt the shudder that went through him, heard the sudden increase in the rate of his heartbeat and her own heart leapt in response. The aching longing threatened to drive her out of her mind and she pressed close up against him without fear or reservation. Her feelings were so real, so right, this was the moment for which she had been born.

With a muffled groan Nick turned to her, gathering her to him and pressing his mouth to hers with a savage tenderness that made her senses reel. His lips tasted faintly of the brandy he had drunk but Erin knew that no alcohol could intoxicate her as potently as the touch of his mouth. She yielded willingly to his passion, her hands tangling in the dark mane of his hair.

'God! No!'

Nick twisted violently away to lie on his back, staring up at the ceiling, the muscles in his face and jaw clenched tight. There was a long, fraught silence, then Erin reached out a trembling hand to his face but Nick repulsed her tentative gesture with an angry jerk of his head.

'Don't!' he snarled and she drew back in fright, pressing her hand against her lips as if he had actually bruised it.

Not again! she thought. Dear God, not again!

'What are you doing to me?' Nick muttered unsteadily, still not looking at her. 'You're tearing me to pieces, destroying me.'

'Not me,' Erin whispered, all the hurt and unfulfilled longing she felt sounding clearly in her voice. '*You're* the one who said no! You're the one who's destroying yourself—and me. I *wanted* you to make love to me!'

'I will not take advantage of you!' Nick spoke through clenched teeth. 'I do have some standards, though when I'm with you I come damn near to forgetting all of them. If you weren't a virgin maybe it would be different, but I can't take your innocence and give you nothing in return—and I have *nothing* to give you, Erin. All I have is a name and handful of half-formed memories and it's not enough.'

It's enough for me! Erin wanted to cry. You're all I want! But Nick had turned to face her and the words died on her lips when she saw the bleakness in his eyes.

'This thing you call love,' he said slowly. 'There is something there, I can feel it when I touch you, a fire that burns us up, but that isn't love. I'm not even sure there is any such thing; I don't believe it exists. What we feel is a form of madness, the result of being trapped together like this. People do the craziest things under such conditions. Hostages fall in love with their captors, kidnappers with their victims, but it isn't real, it doesn't last.'

Somewhere, deep down, a tiny part of Erin's mind recognised the ring of conviction in Nick's voice that spoke of some shadow of memory, but it didn't seem to matter any more, nothing mattered at all.

'I tried to stop this happening,' Nick was saying. 'I tried to keep my distance because I knew that if you started to sympathise with me it could be so very dangerous—for you. It didn't work, and I'm sorry, but I will not have it on my conscience that I abused your innocence in such circumstances.'

'Then what am I doing here, in your bed?' Erin asked drearily, each word an effort to speak. Her mind seemed to be swinging violently between loving him all the more for his principles and hating him for sticking to them now when she wanted him so very much. The gentle brush of Nick's hand across her face was an exquisite torment, bringing the tears to her eyes once more.

'I told you, people do the craziest things under these conditions. I'm not quite sure why you're here. Perhaps it's because you were lost and afraid and I wanted to comfort you just as you came to my room when you heard me cry out. Don't ask for any more than that, Erin.'

Why didn't it hurt? Erin wondered. Surely your heart couldn't break without pain? But even as her mind formed the question she knew the answer. What she felt now was the merciful numbness that came with the first shock of a wound which would ultimately prove unbearable. All Nick felt for her was pity; pity for a foolish, naïve girl who had let her feelings run away with her. Her impetuous declaration of love had brought this bitter humiliation on her.

'I'd better go,' she said forlornly and felt Nick's arms tighten, restraining her.

'Stay tonight,' he whispered. 'There's only a few hours of it left anyway. No commitment, no strings, just two lonely people holding each other in the dark.'

With a sense of despair, Erin knew she was weak enough to settle for that, little as it was. The morning would come soon enough and then they would be as far apart as ever, but for tonight she would know the bittersweet joy of having Nick's arms around her, his body close to hers, and she needed him so desperately that she would accept the little he had to give.

For a long time Erin lay awake, listening to the rain that had begun to fall once more drumming steadily on the roof. Nick never spoke again but, even as sleep claimed her, Erin knew that he still lay stiffly awake beside her. She could feel the tension in every inch of his body and sensed that his thoughts kept him very far from sleep.

He must have slept at last, however, and slipped back into the nightmare that had gripped him earlier for when, in the stillness of the dawn, his restless tossing woke Erin from her own shallow doze she heard him moan aloud and call the name Marie over and over again. Only then did she recall the intonation in Nick's voice when he had said 'two lonely people holding each other in the dark', and when she heard the cry of loss and longing that was another woman's name, that was when the protective numbness faded and the pain really began.

CHAPTER TEN

THE first thing that struck Erin when she woke was the silence: not even the faint patter of the rain broke the stillness. She blinked vaguely, confused by the fact that she was not in her own room, then as she stretched lazily her hand touched the space beside her and she jolted upright sharply, remembering. The side of the bed where Nick had lain was empty, only a dent in the pillow showing that he had ever been there. Erin's heart lurched at the thought that the rain might have cleared the snow and Nick might be gone already, going out of her life as mysteriously as he had come into it.

Her fears eased slightly as she stumbled down the stairs to find Nick in the hall then revived again sharply as she took in the fact that he was fastening his coat.

'Where are you going?' The question came out jerkily.

'Out,' Nick replied curtly, the determined line of his jaw warning her not to ask where.

'But you can't go out in this! It's too dangerous!'

'I'll see how far I get. If it's too bad I can always turn back.'

'Oh.' Erin expelled her breath in a long sigh.' You are coming back then?'

'Yes, I'm coming back.' Nick's tone was heavy.' I have to—I've nowhere else to go.'

The next few hours were some of the longest Erin had ever spent. Everything she did seemed to take twice as long as usual and yet when she looked at the clock she found that only minutes had passed and if she paused long enough to think her mind was immediately crowded with images of Nick, driving her to spend long, frustrating times staring out of the window, hoping vainly to see his tall figure, dark against the snow, returning to the cottage.

If only she knew where he had gone, if he really intended to come back! The roads were still treacherous but if Nick was really determined ... Perhaps his promise to come back had only been given to prevent any further protest on her part. When the front door opened at last the sound had her running into the hall, her heart soaring.

The rain had begun again, lashing down this time, and Nick's hair was plastered against his head, his jacket and jeans stained with dark patches. Erin barely had time to register the shadows on his face that revealed how much his expedition had taken out of him before he strode into the kitchen. Only when he had placed the kettle on the stove and lit a flame beneath it did he turn and give Erin a slow, considering look, his eyes lingering on the length of slender leg revealed by the rust-coloured sweater dress she wore.

'That's the first time I've seen you in a skirt,' he drawled softly. 'It's a definite improvement. Do you want coffee?'

Erin could only shake her head in silent refusal for there was something about his face, something indefinable and elusive, that sent a sensation like the slow trickle of icy water down her spine, depriving her of speech.

There had been so many bewildering shifts of mood but this one was different. It was almost as if there was something in the air itself that brushed against Erin's nerve ends and set them quivering like the sensitive antennae of a butterfly, making her feel that Nick was once more as much a stranger to her as the nameless intruder who had appeared in this kitchen three days before.

It was when Nick pulled off his jacket and flung it on

to the table that Erin noticed a new bulkiness about the pockets.

'What's that?' she asked awkwardly with a stiff little gesture in the direction of the coat.

One dark eyebrow quirked upwards and Erin had distinctly ambiguous feelings about the sudden humourless smile that crossed Nick's face and disappeared at once, never having reached his eyes.

'Observant aren't we?' he commented tersely. 'And curious—but remember what curiosity did to the cat, Erin.'

Erin stiffened at his tone. Talking to Nick was like moving across a vast, uncharted minefield. One false move and something was going to blow up right in her face.

'If you don't want to tell me you've only got to say!' she snapped tartly, but Nick had already pulled the jacket roughly towards him and was emptying the pockets.

'Cigarettes,' he said, tossing two unopened packets on to the table.

Erin followed the movement with her eyes, her gaze resting blankly on the gold coloured boxes. So he had made it to the village, she thought slowly, and almost missed Nick's next remark.

'One cheque book, name of Nicholas Hazard.' The cheque book landed beside the cigarettes with a soft thud. 'Driving licence, ditto, with an address in London—oh, and a wallet, a rather full wallet at that, so now I can pay you for the food I've eaten. It's the least I can do. I can never repay you for all you've done but I can make sure you're not out of pocket when I leave.'

'There's no need for that!' Erin spoke automatically, her mind not on her own words but on the things Nick had said. 'You're going?' It came out in a hoarse croak.

'Soon,' Nick agreed. 'Tomorrow maybe. I couldn't get the car to move today.'

Realisation was slowly dawning on Erin's numbed brain. Her eyes went back to the small collection of objects on the table. London, he had said, an address in London. Somewhere there existed a life for Nick beyond the four walls of Moor End Cottage. She should be so happy for him but instead her heart was tearing in half with the realisation that it was as she had feared. As soon as Nick found some clue to himself he was anxious to go, back to the world in which he really belonged, away from her.

'You——' she began.

'I found the car,' Nick finished for her.

As if in a dream Erin reached out and touched the cheque book, running her fingertips over it as if by that slight contact she could absorb something of Nick, learn something about him. London didn't fit, somehow. She couldn't imagine Nick living day after day in a big city—and he'd never got that tan in an English winter.

'Where was it?' she asked with difficulty.

'Just off the road, a mile or two from here. I'd thought it would be further than that but I found the tree I remembered almost at once. I must have wandered round in circles after I fell—and just to put your mind at rest, there was no sign of anyone else having been in the car.'

Erin started guiltily. For the past forty-eight hours she had been too caught up in her own doubts and feelings and had forgotten about that particular problem. Clearly Nick had not.

With his coffee made, Nick flung himself down in a chair and lit a cigarette, drawing on it deeply before picking up the driving licence and studying it throughfully.

'I suppose if I go to this address there'll be someone

there who'll know me,' he said at last and an odd note in his voice brought Erin's eyes swinging round to his face. 'What do you think?'

There it was again, that elusive, unfathomable expression that seemed to catch on every nerve. The blue eyes were hooded, concealing his thoughts, shutting her out.

'You're probably right.'

It was difficult to speak normally because she knew she was trying not to think of who that someone might be. What *would* Nick find in that house—or flat—in London? Was there really a wife and child? Nick had been adamant in his denial of the fact that he was married but he had been so confused at the time that she didn't know what to believe.

'Unless, of course, you live on your own.' It was a vain, foolish hope, but still she had to say it.

'Unlikely don't you think? So far there are at least two candidates for the post of resident mistress—the mysterious Marie and the woman in the photograph, unless they happen to be one and the same person. Still, one of them should be able to tell me a bit about myself.'

'I'm sure they will!' Erin snapped, the searing jealousy that had flashed through her giving her voice an added intensity.

Perversely, having refused Nick's offer of a coffee earlier, Erin now desperately wanted a drink in the hope that its warmth would ease the chill that gripped her heart. She moved to relight the stove, needing to be doing something in order to avoid looking at Nick.

'Shall I make you something to eat?' she offered edgily.

'I'm not hungry.'

'But you've been out for hours! What were you doing all that time?'

'Thinking.' Nick's expression was unyielding; he was giving nothing away.

He shot a swift, sidelong glance at Erin's face, as if assessing her reaction, then turned his attention back to the driving licence in his hand, tapping it restlessly against the table. The slight, persistent sound jarred on Erin's overstretched nerves, fretting at her mind like all the questions that still remained unanswered.

'All right, don't tell me anything!' she exclaimed angrily.

'I won't,' was the unperturbed response. Suddenly Nick's eyes were on her face, disconcertingly direct and challenging. 'What makes you think there's anything to tell?'

'Well there must be!' Erin's pent-up frustration exploded suddenly. 'Are you trying to tell me you found nothing else—just a cheque book and a driving licence?'

'There was nothing else to find, just those, locked in a glove compartment. I'm sorry to disappoint you, but there was no dismembered corpse in the boot, no case full of stolen banknotes, no bombs.' Viciously Nick crushed out his cigarette and stood up. 'I'm going to get changed,' he announced abruptly. 'These things are soaking.'

She should be used to that dark flippancy by now, Erin thought miserably as the door swung to behind Nick, but somehow it seemed even harder to bear when the world Nick belonged to, which had been only a vague shadow on the horizon before, suddenly seemed so much closer. That world had its nucleus in an address in London, an address she didn't even know because Nick hadn't told her and he had taken the driving licence away with him. In London there were people who knew Nick, friends—a lover perhaps.

Erin stared out at the rain, scarcely seeing how the snow shrank away from it rapidly. Each drop of water brought the time when Nick would leave her closer, second by second, and their effect could have been no more devastating to her heart if they had been drops of acid slowly eating her away inside.

If it had been a long, difficult morning, then what remained of the afternoon was even harder to bear. Nick stayed upstairs for an hour or more and when he finally came down, dressed once again in the navy sweater and denim jeans he had worn on the day he had arrived, he was remote and uncommunicative as if he had already taken the first steps on the road to the way of life that was really his.

The clock on the mantelpiece ticked loudly and insistently as if steadily marking the time that remained before Nick's departure. Erin couldn't bear to contemplate any time after that, she couldn't imagine how she would exist after he had gone. Unlike him she had no other life to return to when this temporary imprisonment was over and without Nick she doubted if she would have any life at all.

Nick had warned her not to trust any feelings that developed in the hothouse conditions of the past few days. The tenuous relationship that had grown up between them had been created by circumstances that had forced them into a intimacy that Nick would otherwise have rejected. But a knife twisted deep in Erin's heart at the thought that her feelings went far deeper than the superficial ones Nick had warned her against. She sighed despondently and then wished she hadn't as the faint sound brought Nick's eyes to her face.

'Cheer up, darling,' he said lightly. 'You won't be stuck here much longer. Just listen to that rain—by tomorrow you'll be free to come and go as you please and all this will just be a bad dream.'

Erin almost laughed aloud at the bitter irony of Nick's words. This was a dream all right, but not a bad one. It was a dream of pure happiness such as she had never known before. Tomorrow, after Nick had gone, the nightmare would begin. She had just a few more hours to be with him, see him, love him, before he went out of her life for good. She couldn't let that precious time pass in this constrained, uncommunicative silence.

'Are you definitely going tomorrow?' Erin asked suddenly, not caring if her thoughts and feelings were openly displayed on her face for Nick to read.

'That was my plan.' Nick's tone was non-committal.

'You're sure the rain will clear the snow by then?'

Nick glanced towards the window, assuming an intense interest in the rain that streamed down the pane.

'There seems very little doubt about that,' he murmured wryly. 'I think you can safely assume that tonight will be the last one I'll spend here.'

'Then we ought to do something special!' Erin declared, surprising herself with her own vehemence.

'What exactly did you have in mind?'

'Well, we don't have to be careful with the food any more so we could have a special meal. I've got a bottle of wine somewhere, I'll get that out.'

'Are we celebrating or drowning our sorrows?' Nick asked on a note of irony but Erin met his eyes unflinchingly. She wanted to make this last night something to remember and she was not going to let Nick spoil it. She even managed a smile.

'Neither,' she told him cheerfully.' We're just going to enjoy ourselves. No more siege conditions, no restrictions.'

'None?'

The deliberately taunting note in the silkily spoken word almost destroyed Erin but she plunged on determinedly, deciding it was safer simply to pretend that she hadn't heard.

'So you can shake yourself out of that black mood you've been in all afternoon and make yourself useful! I'm sure you can manage to cook a couple of steaks if you try, and I'll see to the pudding. I have it on good authority that my apple pie is second to none,' she finished enticingly.

Amazingly, Nick responded, his easy chuckle soft and warm, quite unlike the hard, mirthless laugh Erin had come to dread.

'It sounds irresistible,' he said. 'You're a woman of many talents.'

'I have my moments. I realise that apple pie and custard is probably not at all what you're used to in London but . . .' Erin's voice died away as she saw the way Nick was looking at her.

'How do you know what I'm used to?'

Oh, it was hopeless! For a moment Nick had relaxed, then a few careless words and she had lost him again.

'I—I just assumed—a man like you——'

'Don't assume anything, Erin!' Nick said harshly. 'And for God's sake don't say "a man like you". What the hell do you think *is* a man like me?'

Fearfully Erin shrank away from the ferocity of those coldly blazing blue eyes.

'I'm sorry,' she whispered and heard his muffled curse. A moment later he was at her side, not touching her, though he lifted his hand for a second as if he might.

'No, I'm the one who's sorry,' he said quietly. 'I'm too damn touchy For days I've been without a past, shut in by blank walls, and now——'

Nick broke off abruptly and when he spoke again Erin felt sure that he was not pursuing his original line of thought.

'Now I'm taking it out on you. I'm probably bad-tempered because I'm so darned hungry—and don't you dare say I told you so!' he added, grinning suddenly, restoring Erin's confidence with his change of mood.

'I wouldn't dream of it,' she said sweetly, her heart lighter than it had been for days, the elation that bubbled up inside her in response to Nick's smile bringing her alive in a new and gentler way.

'I believe you said something about an apple pie,' Nick reminded her, his tone telling her that he too shared something of the same mood.

'One apple pie coming up, sir!'

A crazy wish to make this last meal together as much like the first they had shared as possible led Erin to insist that they ate by candlelight and when her limited supply of candles was used up and the room was lit only by the glow of the fire she could not bring herself to turn on the lights again.

The half-light seemed appropriate somehow, she thought dreamily as she sat curled up on a cushion on the rug. Nick was a man of darkness, a man of shadows and mystery. He had come to her out of the gathering dusk, it had been in the total blackness of the power cut that she had first felt the faint stirrings of the feeling that she now recognised as her love for him, and in the darkness just before dawn she had declared those feelings without thought of what the harsh light of day might bring. So now it seemed right that their last night together should be spent in the flickering, uncertain light of the fire, all their former tension apparently forgotten in the companionable mood that descended as they shared the last of the wine.

Beyond the thickly curtained windows the wind lashed the trees and the rain swept away the last of the snow that had brought them together so fatefully. Tomorrow, their paths which had crossed so briefly would divide once more, taking Nick far away to the unknown life that was his and leaving Erin alone, but for tonight this was their own special, private world, easy, relaxed, and warm, a memory to treasure when memories were all she had.

'I don't think I shall ever move again,' Nick murmured contentedly, leaning back against a chair and regarding Erin drowsily through half-closed eyes. 'I should never have let you persuade me into having that second piece of pie, but it was just too tempting.'

'The steaks weren't bad either,' Erin smiled and Nick inclined his head in acknowledgment.

'We endeavour to give satisfaction, Ma'am.' He lifted his glass, holding it out towards Erin. 'Any more wine?'

'I think I could squeeze out another glassful.'

She turned towards him, the bottle raised to pour the wine, but as she tilted it Nick slowly moved the glass away from her so that she was forced to move from her cushion in order to fill it. When she finally managed to pour the wine into the glass Erin found that she had been tricked into positioning herself at Nick's side and when she made a move away from him his arm came round her waist, pulling her close and holding her lightly but firmly.

'Relax,' he whispered, feeling her tension. 'I just want to hold you, nothing more, I promise.'

And because it was what she wanted too, because it was all that she needed to make the evening perfect, Erin let herself relax against him, her head on his shoulder, hearing his heart beating beneath her cheek and feeling the gentle touch of his hand in her hair, sliding the silken curls around his long fingers. With a sigh of contentment she banished all thoughts of the morning from her mind, happy to live only for the moment.

For a time they were silent, content just to savour their new-found peace, neither of them willing to break it with unnecessary words, then Nick stirred slightly, his eyes still fixed on the fire, and spoke slowly, almost to himself.

'When I was a child I used to sit by the fire like this,' he said quietly, and at first, lulled by the wine and the warmth of the flames and the strength of Nick's arms around her, Erin didn't recognise the importance of what he had said.

Then the full significance of Nick's words came home to her with a tremor of shock that jolted her out of her dreaming mood. Not daring to speak for fear she might destroy his concentration, she waited tensely to see if he would go on.

'My father used to tell us stories.' Nick stared deep into the burning coals as if he could see images of the scene he was describing in the flames. 'He had an inexhaustible fund of them, myths, legends, tales from history. I always wanted stories of battles, real or imaginary, it didn't matter. I really thought that war was one great exciting adventure full of heroes and deeds of courage and valour.'

Nick laughed suddenly, the harsh, cynical sound shattering the peaceful atmosphere so that Erin cowered against him when she heard it.

'What a bloody little fool I was!' Nick's voice was thick with self-disgust. 'Well, the reality pretty soon disillusioned me!'

He leaned forward, reaching for his cigarettes and the box of matches Erin had used to light the candles, disturbing her so that she sat up, moving slightly away from him. As the match flared brightly Nick caught sight of Erin's face in the brief glow.

'What is it?' he asked sharply. 'Erin, what's wrong?'

'Nothing's *wrong*,' Erin assured him, her mouth curving slightly at Nick's puzzled frown. 'Oh Nick,' she went on softly. 'Don't you know what you said?'

'What I said?' Nick echoed blankly then a look of shocked comprehension crossed his face. The match he was holding snapped between his fingers and the lighted end flew into the hearth where it spluttered and went out.

'You talked about your childhood—about your father—Nick, you remembered something!'

Nick slumped back against the chair, raking a hand through his hair with a swift, violent movement.

'Dear God, so I did,' he said soberly.

'Isn't it wonderful?' Erin's eyes shone with joy in the firelight. 'Can you remember any more? Do you know who you really are?'

'Yes—yes I do.' Nick's tone was strangely lifeless, with none of the excitement Erin would have thought he would feel at such a moment.

'Then you——' Erin broke off in bewilderment as Nick turned to her and she saw his face properly. 'Nick, what is it?' she cried, suddenly and inexplicably fearful.

Nick's sigh was heavy, filled with an aching weariness.

'I suppose you had to know some time,' he said and he seemed to be making an effort to speak as if all his energy had drained from him. He lifted a hand as if to touch Erin's face but let it drop again almost at once, his expression suddenly remote, the few inches separating them somehow an insurmountable barrier.

'Know what, Nick?' Erin asked, making no attempt to hide the tremor in her voice.

'That I haven't been strictly honest with you.'

How long had he known? Just when had he stopped being honest with her? Who *was* this man she had given her heart to? Involuntarily Erin recoiled from Nick, pain and doubt darkening her eyes.

'Oh Erin!' Nick groaned. 'Don't be like that! It's not what you think—I've only known since this morning but I needed some time to adjust. That dream I had, it seemed to unlock things in my head and when I woke up my mind was full of memories. They were disjointed, muddled, but they were there. I was sure then that I knew where I'd left my car, that's why I had to get out and check at once; I was afraid the memory would fade if I didn't. It was exactly where I thought it would be and when I got into the driving seat it was as if I'd opened a door inside my head and everything fell into place—well, almost everything.'

Erin didn't know whether to laugh or cry. She was so happy for Nick and yet so fearful of the effect of his newly-returned memory on herself and she still didn't understand why he had kept it from her. If this had happened to her, the first thing she would have wanted to do was to tell Nick.

But that was because Nick was the man she loved, the man who made everything so much better simply because she shared it with him, while she was only a girl he had met by accident.

'Tell me about yourself,' she said, keeping her voice steady by a supreme effort of will.

'Nick Hazard—Nicholas James Hazard to be precise. Born August ninth, in Oxford, age thirty-three.' The facts came coldly and impersonally, like an automatic recording. 'Television news reporter, lately correspondent with special responsibility for covering the fighting in the Middle East, but you name it and I've been there.'

He had told her of his accident in just this way, Erin recalled, recounting events in that emotionless, objective voice. It had shocked her at the time but now she understood. As a reporter, he was trained to do just that.

'From Beirut to Belfast there isn't a war I've missed, an atrocity I haven't seen. I'm trained to make reports, not judgments, to work with my mind not my heart. If you get involved, your work starts to suffer.'

The emotionless, automatic voice had vanished and in its place was a terrible bitterness that tore at Erin's heart as if every word was a brutal claw. No wonder Nick had called her an innocent! To a man who spent his life in the war-torn countries of the world, her quiet, comfortable existence must seem hopelessly sheltered and unreal.

'Is that what happened? Did you get involved?' The question was only a thin thread of sound but Nick heard it. He turned his head slowly to face her, his eyes shadowed and dull.

'How long can you watch and report and still stay human?' he demanded and the savagery in his voice hurt so much that she almost cried out at the pain of it. 'If you live only in your mind then, slowly, your heart dies.'

Suddenly Nick smiled almost gently but the contrast between that smile and the bleakness of his eyes was unendurable. One long finger touched Erin's cheek and came away with a single tear glistening on its tip; a tear Erin was not even aware of having shed.

'You see, you are an innocent, little one. You can still cry; you still have that release. You talk so confidently of love, loving someone no matter who or what they are—love conquers all! But if you'd seen what I've seen you'd never believe in love again.'

Violently Nick flung his cigarette into the heart of the fire and immediately lit another one. Then he drained the last of his wine and stared broodingly into the empty glass, his fingers clenched so tightly round it that Erin feared the fragile stem might snap under their pressure.

Erin thought she should be inured to the horror of that shockingly humourless laugh, but this time it was as if she had never heard it with such an intensity before.

'Oh don't!' she cried but Nick hadn't heard her.

'It's wonderfully ironic isn't it?' he said. 'For days all I've wanted to do was remember and now that I have I only wish that I could forget.'

The hand around the glass tightened even more and, fearing for Nick's safety, Erin stretched out and uncurled his fingers, taking it from him gently. Nick made no attempt to resist her and when she took his

hand in hers he let it lie passively in her grasp. She
had no words of comfort to offer him, knowing that
anything she could say would be woefully inadequate.
She had wanted him to open up, confide in her, and
now she had what she wanted—and she didn't know
if she could bear it. But perhaps if she could touch
him, hold him, something of what she felt would
reach him.

'Is this what you dreamed about?' she asked after a
long, silent second and Nick nodded slowly.

'I dreamt about the children—the ones with no future.
In Beirut there was a boy—a child—no more than
twelve. He had a gun, he'd taken it from his father's
body. He boasted to me of the men he'd killed—Erin, I
have a nephew that boy's age!'

Erin was close enough to feel the shudder that shook
Nick's body at his memories and tears stung her eyes
but she forced them back. Tears were a self-indulgent
weakness now. Nick needed more from her than that;
she could not break down. She slid her arms around his
shoulders and held him close.

'If you want to tell me I'll listen,' she told him gently
but Nick shook his head almost angrily.

'I can't burden you with it,' he said brusquely.

He would never know how desperately she wanted to
cry out that that wasn't true, that nothing he could do
would ever be a burden to her. She wanted to share
every part of his life, the good and the bad. They were
all part of him and because of that she could bear
anything. But she couldn't say the words. Nick didn't
feel that way about her; she was not the person he could
confide in completely. For his sake she hoped there was
someone with whom he *could* share the nightmares of
his past—Marie perhaps.

'The woman in the photograph, do you remember
her?'

And there was another thing Nick must never know.

He must never guess how much it had cost her to frame the question she did not want him to answer.

Nick's smile was slow and slightly rueful.

'I thought you'd never ask. Her name's Stella. The little boy's called Nicholas too, though he's usually known as Young Nick to differentiate him from Old Nick—his uncle.'

Stella? The word swung round and round in Erin's head. It came as a shock when she had been expecting to hear that other name, the one she had heard Nick call aloud in his sleep.

Dimly she became aware that Nick was watching her closely. He seemed to be waiting for some response— but to what? What had he said? Young Nick ... Old Nick ... his—The realisation lit her face with a joy that shone unrestrainedly in her eyes.

'His uncle!'

'Yes, Erin, not my child but my brother's youngest son. We're always being mistaken for twins, James and I, though he's actually two years older. That's why Nicky looks so much like me, but he isn't mine— unfortunately. He's a lovable little scamp, just the sort of son I'd want. James sent me that picture when I was out in Beirut. I used to carry it everywhere with me as a kind of talisman against the horrors I saw, a symbol of hope, proof that somewhere there was a child with a future. That's where I'd been this weekend, to stay with James and Stella. I was travelling back when the snow started and the car got stuck so I decided to abandon it and try to find somewhere to stay until things improved. I can't have been thinking too straight though, leaving my wallet and things in the car. At some point I slipped and fell—all the rest you know.'

Almost all, that unwanted, rational part of Erin's brain whispered. You haven't told me everything.

'What else do you want to know?' Nick's question made Erin start in shock. She hadn't realised that she had spoken aloud. 'It's Marie, isn't it?' Nick's voice was gentle. 'You want to know who she is. I'd tell you if I could but——' He spread his hands in a gesture of resignation and defeat. 'She's the missing piece of my personal jigsaw puzzle.'

'You don't—you can't——' Erin's tongue was strangely thick and clumsy. She stumbled over her words, unable to get them out.

'I said I remembered almost everything,' Nick reminded her softly. 'Marie and everything about her is the part I can't—or don't want to remember.'

Erin was silent, recalling how, two days before, Nick had said that amnesia was often the result of some emotional shock, something the sufferer couldn't bear to remember. For Nick, Marie was that something— but what could possibly be worse than the things he had already told her?

'Erin.' There was a new note in Nick's huskily hesitant voice, one that spoke of dreams and promises and shared tomorrows. 'I know I promised, but I can't keep that promise any more.'

There was no need to ask what he meant and Erin lifted her face to his, offering her lips for his kiss without any need for further words. She was trembling as Nick's mouth touched hers, softly at first, then with a warm, sensual pressure that dispelled her initial shyness, drove any hesitation from her mind, and she moved with him as he lowered her to the rug, covering her body with his.

There was no haste, no urgency about their lovemaking this time. The magic of their private world enclosed them still and minutes or hours ceased to exist in the sensuous exploration of each other's bodies, touching, stroking, caressing, slowly moving towards the moment of union. Erin was without fear or shame, her movements languid and relaxed as Nick's hands and lips moved over her, rousing those intoxicating sensations in every nerve, finding pleasure spots she had never known existed, until she thought she would faint with the joy of his touch.

At some point their clothes were discarded but even the sudden chill of the night air on her skin did not intrude on the languorous trance that filled Erin's mind and a moment later the warmth of Nick's flesh against her own was a new and devastating delight that made her cry aloud in an ecstasy of longing.

Nick's hands were less gentle now but Erin welcomed his new urgency as she had the softest of caresses, for gentleness no longer satisfied her. She wanted all of him; wanted to know the moment of fulfilment that only his possession could bring. She had no fear of pain though there was a moment when she tensed and cried out. But Nick's mouth brushed the cry from her lips and a second later all pain was gone, swept away on a burning tide of pleasure. Erin's last coherent thought was that now she understood why this act of love was called a consummation. It was a perfect, blazing fire that consumed them both, its heat forging the final indestructible bond between them.

CHAPTER ELEVEN

ERIN hummed softly to herself as she worked at the knitting machine, filled with a sense of contentment that even the drizzling rain outside could do nothing to dispel. The roads were passable now and Nick had gone to collect his car and all of her thoughts were centred on what would happen then.

At some point during the night, when the last of the coals had burned out in the grate, Nick had gathered her up in his arms and carried her upstairs to his bed. The cold touch of the sheets against her skin had woken her and she had turned to him again, seeking him blindly. She had felt Nick's soft kisses on her throat, the enticing patterns his hands traced over her breasts and thighs, and the slow-burning ache had turned to a clamorous need until she had cried out her love for him and heard his own husky whispering of her name before the fires engulfed them once more.

Afterwards, as she lay in a blissful dream-like state, half-way between sleep and waking, Erin thought she heard Nick murmur that perhaps love did exist after all, but sleep overcame her before she could respond and when she woke she was not sure if she had actually heard the words or if it had been only a dream.

The one small flaw in her happiness was that Nick showed no sign of altering his plans. His bag was packed and lay at the foot of the stairs, a mute reminder of the other world to which he belonged. But even that failed to disturb her equanimity for just before he had set out he had taken her in his arms and kissed her hungrily.

'We'll talk about things when I get back,' he promised softly. 'So you'd better do some serious thinking while I'm gone.'

But Erin knew that she was past the point where thinking had any relevance. Her love for Nick was the kind that would last a lifetime and that knowledge gave her the confidence to await his return in a mood of quiet anticipation.

Far sooner than she had expected, she heard the splashing sound of a car travelling through the melting snow and drawing to a halt outside. Her heart soaring, she ran to fling open the door only to stare in confusion at the man who stood on the threshold.

'Hi! Did you hear me coming? Your dad asked me to call and check you were OK.'

She knew his face, a warm, open face with friendly brown eyes, but she had been expecting Nick and, with his dark image in her mind, this other man did not seem quite real to her. Then her eyes went to the battered Mini parked nearby and her mind snapped back into action.

'Geoff, I'm sorry, I wasn't expecting you! Come in at once, out of the rain!'

Geoff followed her into the house, stamping his feet to shake off the muddy snow that clung to his shoes.

'I'd some house calls to make in Forley so I thought I'd see how you were,' he said. 'I brought you a paper so you can catch up on what's been going on in the world while you've been cut off.'

'Thanks.' Erin's response was abstracted. She was testing her feelings, probing her reactions to Geoff to see if there was any hurt left at seeing him like this. There was none, not even a twinge of regret. Nick had cured her of all that.

Carelessly Erin dropped the newspaper on to the hall table, taking Geoff's arm to draw him into the living room.

'Come and get warm—and tell me about married life. How's Becky?'

She listened to Geoff's answer with only half her attention, the other half of her mind straining for the sound of Nick's return. At last her patience was rewarded, she caught the noise of tyres in the snow, the slam of a car door, and leaned back in her seat, a smile warming her face.

'You look so different, Erin,' Geoff was saying. 'There's a new glow about you—I noticed it the moment I came in.'

'I *am* different!' Oh, why didn't Nick come in? He would have seen Geoff's car, but surely that wouldn't make him hesitate? The perfect unity they had reached the night before, the mutual giving and taking of love, could have left him in no doubt that he was the only man in the world for her.

The front door banged in the wind and Erin could stand the waiting no longer. She sprang to her feet, moving towards the door.

'I'm so happy, Geoff, I've met the most wonderful man and . . .'

Her voice trailed off as she stood in the doorway, staring at the empty hall. The newspaper Geoff had brought had fallen from the table and lay untidily on the floor, imprisoning a smaller slip of white paper beneath it, and it took several seconds for Erin to realise that it was in the space where Nick's bag should have been. Dimly she heard the roar of a car engine outside and the sound of a car travelling at a crazy speed in such treacherous conditions.

'No!'

On a cry of pain Erin wrenched open the front door and ran out into the dull, grey morning. Geoff's Mini was still parked by her gate and beside it were the tyre tracks of another, larger car showing clearly in the churned-up mud. As Erin stood in an agony of bruised bewilderment the rain suddenly increased in furty, large, heavy drops splashing on to the ground, blurring the marks of the tyres, obliterating the only sign that Nick had ever existed.

'Who was that?'

Geoff's voice brought Erin back to reality. Slowly she turned and went back into the house, forcing some sort of smile to soothe his evident concern.

'Just someone I wanted you to meet,' she said and was amazed to find that her voice sounded almost normal with only the faintest trace of a tremor that might have been the result of her headlong dash to the door.

'Some other time perhaps.' Geoff was looking at his watch, frowning as he did so. 'I'll have to go, love, but before I do Becky said I was to be sure and give you our phone number. She'd love you to come and have dinner with us sometime, perhaps when you visit your dad at Christmas.'

He had a pen in his hand and was searching in his pockets for something to write on when he spotted the small, crumpled piece of paper on the floor.

'This'll do.'

Picking it up, he scribbled a number on the paper then pinned it on the small noticeboard that hung beside the hall stand.

'I'll meet this superman some other time,' he said. 'I'll look forward to that.'

Then he turned up his coat collar and dashed out into the rain. It was a long time before Erin pulled herself together enough to close the door after him.

Although she knew it was hopeless, Erin checked every room in the house, searching for some sign that it wasn't true or at least something Nick had left behind that would show he meant to come back. But Nick's bedroom was as bare and empty as it had been earlier when he had packed his few personal belongings almost as soon as he had got up. Erin gasped aloud and folded her arms around her body as if to hold herself together. Nick must have planned this all along! Only minutes after leaving the bed in which they had shared such ecstasy, perhaps even as he lay at Erin's side while she dreamed in blind delusion, he had been planning his escape, always meaning to abandon her like this.

Painfully she dragged herself downstairs again. There were no tears in her eyes; to cry you had to be capable of feeling and Erin's heart was dead, shattered into tiny pieces inside her. She had deceived herself into believing that the passion of the night had been a sign of love because she had wanted to believe it could be so, but Nick had given her no cause for such foolish delusions. He had never said he loved her, had said he did not know what love was, and now she knew she could not delude herself any more.

The newspaper Geoff had brought still lay on the hall floor. Wearily Erin picked it up, glancing automatically at the headlines. 'Further Fighting In Beirut ... Fresh Fears For Hostages' Safety ... Car Bomb Explodes In Belfast.'

'Peace on Earth, goodwill to all men.'

Nick's voice sounded so clearly in Erin's mind that for a second she almost believed he stood behind her. She had actually swung round before the illusion faded like the dream it was. Violently she flung the paper from her, sinking down on the bottom stair, hunching her shoulders against the world and trying to find a reason to go on living.

A cold, sneaking wind blew in Erin's face as she alighted from the bus in the village and began the lonely walk back to Moor End. There was little sign of life in the narrow main street and a stray cat perched on the bonnet of a sleekly powerful car that was parked outside Forley's one public house was the only other living creature that had ventured out into the gloom of the January afternoon.

Erin sighed deeply. She should be feeling happy and satisfied; the trip into Bradwood had been particularly successful, she had a file full of orders for more of her designs, but that thought did nothing to cheer her despondent mood. She felt tired and dispirited after the lengthy bus ride during which she had done nothing but stare gloomily out of the window, ignoring the newspaper she had bought on an uncharacteristic impulse, probably simply because it did not carry the headlines she had come to dread. When Nick had left her she had thought she would never see his face again but for days now it seemed that she had been unable to pass a newsagent's shop without being bombarded by images of the man who still haunted her dreams.

Because it was one of the main news items of the day, there had been plenty of talk about the negotiations to free the three Britons, a missionary doctor and his wife and daughter, taken hostage by Lebanese guerillas almost two months before. Erin had heard her father and Elaine discussing the story several times over the Christmas holiday but with her mind dulled by her own private unhappiness she had taken in few of the details and so was totally unprepared for the devastating moment when, over dinner with Geoff and Becky, she had learned that there had originally been four hostages.

'But you must have known!' Geoff had exclaimed when she had questioned him. 'Even Becky knows about Nick Hazard's involvement in all this, and she's no interest in current affairs at all.'

Erin sat bolt upright in her chair, shock widening her eyes.

'H-Hazard?' she stammered. 'Was that the name you said?'

'That's right, Nick Hazard—one of the best reporters they've got. He'd gone to interview Henderson and was captured with him, but he managed to escape, God knows how, and brought the story back. He'd been living rough for days and looked in a pretty bad way. I should imagine being held prisoner must have been hellish for him, he's not the sort of man who'd take too kindly to being cooped up for days on end.'

Memories were stabbing at Erin like red-hot knives and she clenched her hands into tight fists as Geoff went on.

'Hazard was on leave in England just before Christmas but from what I hear he's out there again now—and right in the thick of things. It seems he's the only one the guerrillas will negotiate with because he won their respect when he was their prisoner. The fellow's got nerve, I must say, but then risks are part of his life. War correspondents are a breed apart.'

'They work with their minds, not their hearts.' Erin spoke mechanically, the words were etched into her brain, she had heard them a million times over in her thoughts since the day Nick had first uttered them.

'And they get high on the danger,' Geoff said, nodding agreement. 'So they can't settle to an ordinary life afterwards. Take Hazard, for example. From all acounts he's a real ladykiller with a string of broken hearts behind him. Love 'em and leave 'em, that's his philosophy. It's the life that makes them hard I suppose, if they weren't like that to start with.'

The next day Erin had fled back to the sanctuary of her cottage, trying to bury herself in her work but ending up spending long hours staring at her drawing board, her body existing in the cold of an English winter while her mind was hundreds of miles away in the heat and danger of Beirut, with Nick. She resolutely avoided all newspaper and radio reports of the hostage story, finding the mere mention of Nick's name too painful to bear, and never once switched on the portable television that had been her father's Christmas present—until the night of New Year's Day.

That night she had abandoned all pretence of work and settled instead for the novelty of watching the evening film, carefully switching on only when it was due to start. But, unknown to Erin, events had been moving rapidly. Early that morning the hostages had finally been released, the evening news had been specially extended to cover the story and when the picture on the set came into focus she found herself looking straight at Nick.

Erin's heart contracted in joy and pain. Just to see Nick was a delight so mixed with anguish that she could not take in a word of the inteview but simply let her eyes rest hungrily on the face of the man she loved like a starving person suddenly offered a banquet.

This then was Nick Hazard. Not the confused and tormented man who had come to her out of the snowstorm, nor the lover, gentle and tender, who had made her his finally and forever, but a hard, capable man in full control of his situation and, to judge by the aloof expression in those vividly blue eyes, a man impatient at any restriction on his freedom. With the sun warming his tanned skin and glinting on the glossy dark hair, he had never looked so vibrantly alive and Geoff's phrase 'high on danger' rang tormentingly in Erin's head.

Nick's experiences had almost destroyed him, his mind rejecting the memory of what he was forced to watch but could not alter, but now it seemed the scars left by those experiences had taken no time at all to heal. Like an addict, Nick had gone back to the world he knew, back to the danger, to the thrill of life lived on a knife-edge of fear, without a thought for her. Love 'em and leave 'em, Geoff had said, but Erin knew that love was not a word that existed in Nick Hazard's vocabulary. He had not loved her; she was just another in the string of broken hearts he had left behind him in the pursuit of ambition and excitement.

The interview finished, Nick was turning away when a camera moved in for a close-up and in that impatient gesture she had seen so many times before he pushed his hand through his hair, brushing it away from his forehead. Erin's breath caught in her throat as she saw the thin, silvery line on his skin where the jagged cut had been and she wondered hopelessly whether he ever remembered how he had come by that faint scar and perhaps, just for a moment, he thought of her.

'And now we're going back to the airport where Doctor Henderson has agreed to hold a press conference.' The impersonal voice of the newsreader broke in on Erin's thoughts but she had had enough. It took only a second to switch off the television but that was long enough to hear the words that seemed to echo round the room long after the screen was blank.

'Well, of course Nick's a hero to my daughter. Marie worships him. I believe she's madly in love with him.'

So now she knew. She need look no further for the reasons for Nick's sudden departure. There was no need to wonder any more about the identity of the girl he had called out to in his dreams. It was no wonder Nick had not been able to listen to that news broadcast; subconsciously he had known that he would learn that the woman he cared about was still held prisoner. The final piece of the jigsaw puzzle was in place, the answer to all the unsolved questions summed up in two words—Marie Henderson.

The sky was growing darker and heavier as Erin

rounded the bend into the dirt track that led to Moor
End and she shivered, pushing her hands deep into her
coat pockets. It had been on just such an evening as this
that Nick had stumbled into her home and into her
heart. How long would it be before she could approach
the cottage and not think of the time when she had
found him asleep in the room upstairs? Would the
memory ever fade or would it return to haunt her on
every winter evening for the rest of her life?

Well, at least Rufus had stayed inside where she had
left him this time, Erin thought with a twinge of sadness
then gave a heartstopping gasp of shock as the door
swung slowly open when she pushed her key into the
lock. It was sticking worse than ever; she would have to
get it seen to before she had a genuine intruder. She
might not be as lucky as she had been with Nick
another time—or did she mean unlucky? Erin abandoned the question as insoluble and, not bothering to
remove her coat, headed for the living room.

The banked-up coals glowed welcomingly and Erin
gave a sigh of contentment as a blast of warm air
greeted her then froze in horror as a faint sound of
movement drew her attention to the tall figure standing
in the shadows beside the fire.

'You left the door unlocked again,' Nick said quietly.
'Don't you ever learn?'

'No!'

The cry sprang from Erin's lips as she flung up a
hand to ward off the tormenting illusion. It had to be
an illusion! Nick could not be here, he was still out in
the Middle East somewhere. She heard the click of a
switch and the room was suddenly flooded with light—
and he was still there, dark and self-assured in a grey
leather jacket and black trousers, big and powerful and
dangerously real.

'Good afternoon, Erin,' Nick said pleasantly. 'I
rather think we've played this scene before, or

something very like it.'

'So we have.' Erin's shock was turning swiftly to anger. 'And that time I made the fatal mistake of not getting rid of you at once; I won't be quite so foolish this time!'

With her head held stiffly high she marched to the door and flung it open.

'Get out of my house, Nick!' she ordered tautly. 'I don't want you here, so please go.'

To her horror, Nick merely shook his head and installed himself in an armchair, lighting a cigarette with the air of a man very much at ease and determined to stay just as long as it pleased him.

'I'm warning you, if you're not out of here by the time I count to ten I'll——'

'You'll do what, Erin?' The steely, blue-eyed gaze belied Nick's casual drawl. 'Have you got a knife in your pocket again or do you plan on something a little different this time? Whatever it is, I suggest you make sure you can use it. You weren't exactly successful the last time if I remember rightly.'

Did he have to remind her of that? Erin slumped against the door in defeat, her fury evaporating as swiftly as it had come, leaving her weak and frightened. Without the shield of anger to protect her from her own feelings she was far too vulnerable. If she had, however improbably, actually persuaded Nick to go while she was still in a state of shock then she might have managed to survive at least until he was out of the house. But now, after only a few minutes, her defences had been stripped away and she was totally at the mercy of her love for him.

'Why don't you come and sit down?' Nick said sharply. 'You're behaving like a sulky child and I'm not feeling exactly patient. I'm tired, I've been travelling for over twenty-four hours. The least you could do is to try to be a little more gracious in your welcome.'

'Gracious! Welcome!' Erin repeated with bitter sarcasm 'You haven't got the point, Nick. You're *not* welcome so you can just get in your car and go.'

'My car isn't here. I left it in the village and walked the rest of the way.'

Erin had a sudden mental image of the car she had seen, its sleekly powerful lines somehow alien in Forley's main street. She should have known! Some sixth sense should have alerted her. She swallowed hard, trying to dredge up some of the anger she needed.

'Well you can walk right out again! You——'

'For God's sake, come and sit down!' Nick broke in impatiently. 'You look ridiculous hovering there like some avenging angel! Take your coat off, sit down, and let's try and talk this out in some sort of civilised manner.'

'Civilised is not a word I'd use to describe you!' Erin retorted, but she did as he said just the same; she didn't fancy Nick's reaction if she disobeyed him. 'What are you doing in Yorkshire anyway?' she demanded when the silence between them threatened to grow unnerving.

Nick turned his head slowly to look at her, his gaze disturbingly steady. 'Looking for somewhere to live,' he said quietly.

It was the last thing she'd expected.

'But why? You're hardly in this country long enough to make it worth the expense of keeping a flat in London, let alone a house way up here. Your work takes you abroad most of the time.'

'Not any more. I decided it was time for a change. Spending ten months of the year out of the country, not knowing where I'll be next year, next month even, only works if you've no ties. It's no life for a married man.'

Erin's blood ran cold. She was suddenly intensely

grateful for the fact that she was sitting down, doubting that her legs would have had the strength to support her if she had been standing.

'You're getting married?' she croaked painfully.

'Thinking of it,' was the laconic reply.

'Who——' Erin couldn't get the question out. 'Who's the lucky girl?' she managed in a rush. 'Marie Henderson?'

'Good Lord, no!' Nick's laughter was a warm, rich sound, his amusement genuine. 'An interesting thought but no, not Marie.'

'Someone else then?'

Nick's silent nod started Erin off on a new and intensely painful train of thought. Had she been wrong in her belief that Marie Henderson was the woman Nick really cared about, the woman he had abandoned her so callously for? It was little more than a month since she had first heard Nick speak Marie's name, only days since Doctor Henderson had announced to the world that his daughter was madly in love with Nick Hazard—and here he was calmly talking about marrying someone else without a sign of guilt or embarrassment. Did he have no conscience at all where women were concerned?

'Moor End's just the sort of place I've been looking for,' Nick said thoughtfully. 'I've had enough of London and I have this crazy ambition to write—it might exorcise a few ghosts. I feel I could write here. What do you think?' He directed the question at Erin with disconcerting abruptness.

'I don't know!' Erin snapped, her self-control on the verge of collapsing altogether. 'Why ask me?'

'Who else would I ask?' Nick came back at her softly.

'Why, your—the girl you're going to marry, of course!' Oh, how it hurt to say that! 'Surely she's got some say in the matter?'

'Of course,' Nick agreed smoothly. 'But she doesn't seem prepared to give me an answer.'

Erin shook her head in angry confusion. Nick was talking in riddles—and it was *her* house he was talking about!

'You've already told her you want to live at Moor End?' she spluttered indignantly.

'No more than a minute ago,' was the bewilderingly flippant reply.

'Nick, stop making fun of me! That's impossible and you know it! You couldn't have told her only a minute ago because . . .'

Erin's voice failed her completely and she jolted upright in shock. He couldn't mean what she thought! There was no way he could mean that!

'Because,' Nick prompted, his eyes never leaving her face. 'Keep going, Erin, you'll get there in the end.'

'Because—because you were talking to me.'

The words came in a painful gasp. It was too cruel! How could he torment her like this when she knew he didn't mean a word he said! A thought struck her with the force of a physical blow—Nick had always resorted to this evasive sort of humour when he was talking about something that meant a great deal to him! She glanced at Nick sharply and saw from his expression that he had read her thoughts in her eyes.

'Exactly,' he said, leaning back in his chair with a sigh of satisfaction. 'So now will you answer me? Do you think we could live at Moor End after we're married?'

'But we're not going to be married!'

'We're not?' For the first time Nick's voice held a note of uncertainty. 'For God's sake, Erin, why not?'

'You know damn well why not! Do you think I'd

marry you after what you did to me? You walked in here out of the blue, took over my life, blasted it apart, then handed me back the pieces and disappeared without so much as a goodbye!'

'There wasn't time——' Nick began, but Erin swept aside his interjection.

'I didn't know where you were or what you were doing; everything I learned I got from the papers or the television like millions of other people all over the country—I never heard a word from you! And now you turn up again as cool as you please and talk about marriage as if it was all decided. Well it isn't! I wouldn't marry you if you were the last man on earth!'

'You told me once that you loved me,' Nick put in quietly, taking all the fight out of her in one swift rush. 'Wasn't that true?'

Erin bent her head and hid her face in her hands so that Nick would not see the weak, defeated tears that streamed down her cheeks.

'I was a different person when I said that,' she told him, her voice muffled by her concealing fingers. 'I was stupid, emotional, and, as you were at such pains to point out, frighteningly naïve. I know better now, I've grown up—you made me grow up! You taught me that love isn't enough, that it doesn't bring about the happy ending to the fairy tale. It took a while to sink in I admit, I'm afraid I'm rather a slow pupil, but you—you're a damn good teacher!'

'Erin, no!'

With a swift, lithe movement Nick was out of his chair and kneeling on the floor before her. Gently but firmly he prised her hands away from her face and held them so that she had no protection from his searching eyes.

'Erin, my darling, please don't! Don't deny your love, not now, when I've come to realise it can exist and know that I can feel it, too.'

Twice Erin opened her mouth to speak and both times her voice refused to form the words she so desperately wanted to say. But Nick seemed to sense her need intuitively and there was no hesitation in his own voice when he answered her unspoken question.

'Yes, I love you. I love you so much that I've just thrown up my job and travelled half-way across the world just to tell you that.'

There was no defensive humour now, only an open, unrestrained sincerity that matched the fires burning in his eyes, giving Erin the strength to find her voice at last.

'But you said you didn't believe in love.'

'I know I did, and at the time I meant what I said—I was still working with my head instead of my heart. Rationally I didn't believe that anyone could love like that after only three days—and in those circumstances. But that night, when I made love to you, it was as if no other woman had ever existed, as if the world and all its sordid brutality had suddenly ceased to be and all there was was you. With your innocence and your unselfishness you gave me so much. You gave me hope, something to balance in the scales against the evil I saw every day, and I knew I couldn't go on unless I had your love to give me the strength I needed. These past few weeks have been hell without you. I couldn't contact you, I wasn't even in civilisation until yesterday—but you were always there, in my mind, and when things got tough I thought of you and dreamed of the time when it would all be behind me and I could come back and ask you to marry me.'

Nick's mention of his four week absence made Erin shift uneasily in her seat.

'Then why did you go like that?' she asked, her voice

very low, and Nick moved to sit beside her, still retaining her hands in his.

'Didn't you read the paper your friend brought you?' he asked softly and Erin turned a puzzled face towards him.

'What has that got to do with it?'

'Everything. It's a long story, Erin, and not a particularly easy one to tell.'

'I'll listen,' Erin assured him, all her heart in her words. 'I've got plenty of time.' And she had, all the time in the world, for she knew that her entire future rested on what Nick was going to say.

'I had to leave because of Marie,' Nick began and instantly Erin stiffened, all her fears flooding back.

So she had been right to suspect there was something between Nick and the Hendersons' daughter! But if that was so, how could he tell her that he loved her? She felt as if she had been given the world only to have it snatched back almost at once.

'Erin, you don't understand! You can't understand. You'd never have asked if I was going to marry Marie if you'd had the slightest idea of the truth. Look——'

Nick twisted round and pulled the newspaper Erin had brought in with her from under her coat. Without hesitation he turned to the centre pages and held them open for her to see.

'That's Marie, you crazy idiot! Look at her and tell me you're still jealous.'

Following the direction of his pointing finger, Erin stared at the blurred and grainy photograph. It showed Nick on his arrival back in England on the previous day but his face was partially obscured, hidden behind the bright golden hair and ecstatically beaming smile of a deliriously happy but very young child.

'Marie's only six years old.' Nick's voice held none of the reproach that Erin knew she deserved. 'She went through hell when she and her parents were captured but she never complained. She had more courage than any of us and she put up with the most appalling conditions without a murmur. It was for her sake that I took the gamble of trying to escape and when I did manage to get away I vowed I'd get her out too if it was the last thing I did. It was a very dodgy situation for a while but then things seemed to calm down. The official negotiations were making steady progress and I thought I wasn't needed any more— that's when I came back to England. I went to York to visit James in the belief that the Hendersons would be free any day, but then I got a phone call telling me that negotiations had broken down. The guerrillas refused to talk to anyone but me and they threatened to kill Marie if I wasn't there in twenty-four hours. I drove like a maniac to get back to London but I hadn't bargained on the worst snowfall in fifty years.'

'You were on your way to London when you ended up here?'

Nick nodded silently, his eyes darkening at the memory.

'That bang on the head drove everything from my mind but I suppose, underneath it all, I knew I'd missed the deadline. Subconsciously I believed Marie must be dead and that was too unbearable to contemplate so I couldn't remember. Then when I came back from fetching the car I found that newspaper, that told me that by some miracle the guerrillas had agreed to extend the deadline and Marie was still alive—but, of course, by then they couldn't find me. I had to go, I couldn't let Marie down again, I could only pray you'd understand. I just had time to scribble that note—a proper explanation would have taken too long. Every second was vital so I couldn't even come into the room in case you kept me.'

'What note?' Erin said sharply. 'I never saw one.'

'So that's what all this has been about! Erin, believe me, I left one. I put it on top of the newspaper, I felt sure you'd see it there—Erin, where are you going?'

But Erin was already out of the door. The few seconds it took to cross the hall were some of the longest of her life, then she had the paper with Geoff's phone number on it in her hands, hands that shook uncontrollably as she turned it over.

'Erin, please trust me. I'll explain everything as soon as I can. Until then—I love you. Nick.'

'I love you.' Even at a time when the smallest second mattered, Nick, the man who had said he didn't believe in love, had snatched a few extra moments to write those words!

Through her tears Erin saw Nick's tall figure in the doorway. Beyond speech, she held up the hastily written note, her heart and all the love that was in it displayed openly in her eyes. Without a word Nick opened his arms to her and she flung herself into them, hiding her face against his chest, letting her tears wash away the bitterness, the anger and the hurt that had been stored up inside her.

Nick let her cry until she was calm, holding her close all the time, his hand stroking her hair in a gentle, soothing movement. Then as her sobs ceased he gathered her up in his arms and carried her through into the living room, laying her carefully on the settee and settling himself on the floor beside her. He leaned across her to place one hand on either side of her face, his blue eyes lovingly intense.

'Now perhaps I can get an answer to my question,' he said softly. 'Will you—no!' He stopped himself abruptly. 'Let me rephrase that—*when* will you marry me?'

'Don't I get a proper proposal?' Erin teased in a voice that was slightly unsteady and Nick shook his head firmly.

'No chance. I'm not taking no for an answer, so why bother to ask? Now tell me—*when*?'

'When do you want me?' Erin's voice was stronger now, her smile deliberately provocative, and she saw the fire that lit deep in Nick's eyes in response.

'I want you for ever. Today, tomorrow, next week, next year, but most of all I want you *now*!' he groaned.

'Good,' Erin whispered, drawing him down against her, her lips seeking his. 'Because I want you, too, my darling. I want you so very much.

A long, long time later, when Nick's mouth left hers to trail soft kisses down her throat, Erin sighed, stretching luxuriously, her whole body one warm glow of contentment.

'What a pity we're not snowed in any more,' she murmured languorously. 'I can think of nothing I'd like better than to spend the next few days—a week at least—alone with you with the guarantee of no interruptions.'

Nick's chuckle was a sound of pure delight.

'Have you looked out of the window since you got back?' he whispered against her hair. 'Because I rather suspect you're going to get your wish. It's snowing harder than it was the day I first arrived.'

'Is it?'

Erin tried to sit up to see but Nick's arms came round her tightly, restraining her.

'Later!' he growled. 'Right now we have more important things to do. Let the weather do what the hell it likes, now that I'm here with you. It can throw a blizzard for all I care, I'll keep you safe and warm.'

Surrendering herself to his embrace with a sigh of pure happiness, Erin knew that Nick's words were a promise not just for the present but for the rest of her life.

Harlequin Romance

Coming Next Month

Available in September wherever paperback books are sold,
or through Harlequin Reader Service.

In the U.S.   In Canada
P.O. Box 1397   P.O. Box 2800, Postal Station A
Buffalo, N.Y.   5170 Yonge Street
14240-1397   Willowdale, Ontario M2N 6J3

Could she find love as a mail-order bride?

MARIANNE WILLMAN

PIECES OF SKY

In the Arizona of 1873, Nora O'Shea is caught between life with a contemptuous, arrogant husband and her desperate love for Roger LeBeau, half-breed Comanche Indian scout and secret freedom fighter.

Shay Flanagan is Gypsy,
the raven-haired beauty who inflamed passion
in the hearts of two Falconer men.

Carole Mortimer

GYPSY

Lyon Falconer, a law unto himself, claimed Shay—when he didn't have the right. Ricky Falconer, gentle and loving married Shay—when she had no other choice.

Now her husband's death brings Shay back within Lyon's grasp. Once and for all Lyon intends to prove that Shay has always been—will always be—*his* Gypsy!

Harlequin "Super Celebration"
SWEEPSTAKES

NEW PRIZES—NEW PRIZE FEATURES & CHOICES—MONTHLY

1. To enter the sweepstakes, follow the instructions outlined on the Center Insert Card. Alternate means of entry, NO PURCHASE NECESSARY, you may also enter by mailing your name, address and birthday on a plain 3" x 5" piece of paper to: In U.S.A.: Harlequin "Super Celebration" Sweepstakes, P.O. Box 1867, Buffalo, N.Y. 14240-1867. In Canada: Harlequin "Super Celebration" Sweepstakes, P.O. Box 2800, 5170 Yonge Street, Postal Station A, Willowdale, Ontario M2N 6J3.

2. Winners will be selected in random drawings from all entries received. All prizes will be awarded. These prizes are in addition to any free gifts which might be offered. Versions of this sweepstakes with different prizes may appear in other presentations by TorStar and their affiliates. The maximum value of the prizes offered is $8,000.00. Winners selected will receive the prize offered from their prize package.

3. The selection of winners will be conducted under the supervision of Marden-Kane, an independent judging organization. By entering the sweepstakes, each entrant accepts and agrees to be bound by these rules and the decision of the judges which shall be final and binding. Odds of winning are dependent upon the total number of entries received. Taxes, if any, are the sole responsibility of the entrant. Prizes are not transferable. This sweepstakes is scheduled to appear in Retail Outlets of Harlequin Books during the period of June 1986 to December 1986. All entries must be received by January 31st, 1987. The drawing will take place on or about March 1st, 1987 at the offices of Marden-Kane, Lake Success, New York. For Quebec (Canada) residents, any litigation regarding the running of this sweepstakes and the awarding of prizes must be submitted to La Regie de Lotteries et Course du Quebec.

4. This presentation offers the prizes as illustrated on the Center Insert Card.

5. This offer is open to residents of the U.S., and Canada, 18 years or older, except employees of TorStar, its affilliates, subsidiaries, Marden-Kane and all other agencies and persons connected with conducting this sweepstakes. All Federal, State and local laws apply. Void where prohibited or restricted by law. Winners will be notified by mail and may be required to execute an affidavit of eligibility and release which must be returned within 14 days after notification. Winners consent to the use of their name, photograph and/or likeness for advertising and publicity in conjunction with this and similar promotions without additional compensation. One prize per family or household. Canadian winners will be required to answer a skill testing question.

6. For a list of our most recent prize winners, send a stamped, self-addressed envelope to: WINNERS LIST, c/o Marden-Kane, P.O. Box 525, Sayreville, NJ 08872.

No Lucky Number needed to win!

HARLEQUIN HISTORICAL

Explore love with Harlequin in the Middle Ages, the Renaissance, in the Regency, the Victorian and other eras.

Relive within these books the endless ages of romance, set against authentic historical backgrounds. Two new historical love stories published each month.

HIST-A-1